"I don't want someone to marry me for my money."

Cindy held her breath.

"That's why I need your help," Parker continued. "Would you…? I need you to make me into the kind of guy your sister could fall in love with."

The life went out of her.

"I need you to turn me into a stud."

He'd rendered her speechless. He was so intent, he didn't even notice that his statement crushed all her hopes….

Val Daniels wrote her first romance in the sixth grade when her teacher told the class to transform a short story they'd read into a play. Val changed the bear attack story into a romance and should have seen the writing on the wall. She didn't. An assortment of jobs, hobbies and businesses later, Val stumbled across a *Writer's Market* in the public library and finally knew what she wanted to be when she grew up. She suspects it will take eighty or ninety years to become bored with this career.

Val lives in Kansas with her husband, two children and a Murphy dog. She welcomes correspondence—with a SASE—from readers at P.O. Box 113, Gardner KS 66030, U.S.A.

Making Mr. Right
Val Daniels

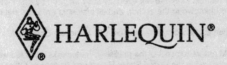

HARLEQUIN®

TORONTO • NEW YORK • LONDON
AMSTERDAM • PARIS • SYDNEY • HAMBURG
STOCKHOLM • ATHENS • TOKYO • MILAN • MADRID
PRAGUE • WARSAW • BUDAPEST • AUCKLAND

ISBN 0-373-03563-2

MAKING MR. RIGHT

First North American Publication 1999.

CHAPTER ONE

CINDY'S brush stopped making soapy circles on the cement floor. The pair of battered running shoes that had stepped into her view gave Parker Chaney away, so she wasn't surprised to see his devastating smile aimed at her when she looked up.

"What are you doing?" he asked as if he'd seen her only yesterday.

"Trying to get this stain out," she said in the same nonchalant tone, though her heart was thumping in triple time. She wished he'd at least *act* thrilled. After six weeks with nothing but a few brief phone calls, couldn't he at least pretend seeing her was noteworthy?

A mixture of irritation and the desire to make the occasion memorable got the best of her. She swiped the brush across the toes of his grungy shoes, careful not to spray the legs of his business suit with her sudsy water.

He jumped away. "What are you doing?" His tone was totally different this time.

"You already asked that," she reminded him, pitching her scrub brush at the pail of cleaning water. Drying her wet hands on the legs of her jeans, she stood. "What are *you* doing?" Darn it. Only pride kept her from throwing her arms around him and revealing *how* delighted she was to see him. Finally.

Parker scratched the side of his head, leaving a

sprig of dark hair standing on end. The gesture helped him think.

"I need your help," he admitted, letting his meditative scowl deepen.

"Oh?" She crossed her arms to keep from pressing the hair standing on end back in place. What else was new? "Helping" Parker usually meant he needed a sounding board, someone to listen to one of his new ideas—not that she usually understood them.

He got right to the point, also as usual. "I think it's time I got married."

But usually, his point didn't make Cindy's heart stop. It jumped to her throat then sped to a pace that would have kept up with a freight train. *What'd you say?* The question ran through her head but she couldn't have gotten her mouth around a word if her life depended on it.

"Don't you?" he asked, continuing as if the subject of marriage was a normal conversation for him. "I'm thirty-three years old. I tend to get too wrapped up in things. I've been thinking that if I don't get married soon, I'll find myself old, no kids, no family, all my chances gone."

Her mouth still hung open. She had to consciously force herself to close it. "Don't worry, PC. If things get that desperate," she finally managed, "you can always find someone who'll marry you for your money." No problem making the comment as dry as she wanted, either. Her mouth was imitating a desert.

"Funny." The look he shot her said he thought she was amusing, despite the fact he didn't like what she'd said. It was too true.

As if money was the only thing he had! He was brilliant. His name was uttered with reverence in computer circles. Financial experts raved about him and delightedly recommended buying stock in his company. But she'd said his name in the same worshipful way long before his "miraculous" rise to success. She loved him despite the money.

She'd loved him when he was dirt poor and living next door to her family in their old neighborhood. She'd still be there, if it wasn't an industrial park now.

She considered the destruction of their neighborhood the worst thing that had ever happened to her. Blocks and blocks of it had been razed to make way for "progress." They'd all had to move. Until that time, almost six years ago, she'd seen Parker on a daily basis. Now she had to rely on seeing him whenever he got the whim...as he seemed to have now. Pride kept her from calling him when he'd go a couple of months ignoring their friendship.

She longed to touch him, smooth the unruly, needing-a-trim haircut back into place. She wanted to push into his space, lift her lips for a kiss, make him uncomfortably aware of her nearness. Unfortunately he probably wouldn't notice. Or be uncomfortable. She settled for a friendly hug.

He hugged her back then sobered as his one-track mind got back to the reason for finally putting in an appearance in her life. "I don't want someone to marry me for my money, Cindy." His expression turned even more earnest, if that was possible.

Cindy held her breath.

"That's why I need your help," he continued. "Would you...I need you to make me into the kind of guy Mallory could fall in love with?"

The life went out of her.

"I need you to turn me into a stud."

He'd rendered her speechless. He was so intent, he didn't even notice that his statement crushed her. She looked down quickly in case he came out of his hazy little myopic world long enough to see that tears had sprung to her eyes. She couldn't think of anything to say or do except return to scrubbing the floor.

She resumed her position on her hands and knees and dumped a splash of the warm, strong ammonia-scented water on the cement floor.

Parker sprang out of the way again as the small wave surged toward his feet. "What *are* you doing?"

"What does it look like," she said irritably. "I'm washing the floor."

"But why?"

"To get this oil spot out," she said. "Out damn spot!" she mumbled at it. Quoting Shakespeare gave her an excuse to cuss, even though she almost choked over the huge lump that had taken residence in her throat.

Darn him, what did he want with Mallory? Surely in all this time, he'd gotten over her. He hadn't seen her for almost twelve years. She'd been married twice. Why? Why? Wh—

"Since when have you worried about oil spots on the garage floor?" Parker asked. "You've never exactly been Miss Tidy."

"Tidier than my sister," she muttered and then cursed the floor under her breath.

"What?"

"I'm almost ready to put this house on the market," she said loudly. "My car's been leaking oil like there's no tomorrow and an oil spot is the kind of thing that mars the image and subconsciously lessens the value for some people. If I take care of the little details," she quoted by habit since it had almost become her motto, "I usually get my price."

His smile broadened. "And that's exactly why I need you. You'll take care of all the little details. Just consider me your next fixer-upper. I know you can do it—even if you're not going to get that spot out that way."

"Oh?" She stood, hands on hips, her brush dripping smelly warm water down the leg of her jeans. She barely noticed. She didn't care. "And how would you clean it, Mr. Expert," she asked sweetly.

"You need cat litter and soda."

"Baking soda?"

"Pop. The fizzy carbonated stuff."

"Any particular brand?"

He scowled, thinking. "I don't think so. I heard it on some do-it-yourself show on TV. I don't remember them mentioning any particular brand."

"Well, I have an idea. Why don't you clean it if you know so much about it." Actually she didn't doubt he knew what he was talking about. Parker collected little tidbits of meaningless data and spouted them on demand, like one of his computers.

"Sounds like a fair trade." He grinned his charming, boyish grin. The one that always disarmed her. "I'll get the oil stain out of your garage floor, you change me from a frog into a prince."

"For Mallory." Her voice was flat. Skeptical.

The silly grin widened as he nodded.

"When is she going to behold this miraculous transformation," she wondered aloud.

"Oh. I forgot." He reached and checked several pockets before coming up with a piece of paper that had been stuffed in his pants pocket without the benefit of refolding.

She dropped her brush back into her pail, savoring a morbid sense of satisfaction as the ensuing splash reached him and left tiny dark dots on his gray suit pants. He was too absentminded to notice. He pushed his dark rimmed glasses up on his nose with the wrong finger and handed over the paper.

Taking it to the long workbench she'd built across the length of the garage, Cindy smoothed it out.

"A class reunion?" she said, reading the large bold print at the top of the page.

"Yeah." Parker came to stand beside her.

She moved away, suddenly hating his nearness. "What makes you think Mallory will come?"

"Don't you?" He stepped closer again.

She had the last time, Cindy remembered. Their ten-year reunion. Parker had been out of town and extremely disappointed when he'd discovered Mallory had been home while he was gone. He hadn't said another thing about her sister in the intervening five years.

Geminy Christmas! How could he ask her to do this? "She did come the last time," Cindy confirmed. "But I haven't heard a thing from her about this. Surely if she was planning to attend, I would have heard—"

"I just got the invitation today. They were mailed from here. She may not even have hers yet."

Raising both eyebrows, Cindy glanced at her watch, then tilted her head and stared at him. "How long have you been planning this, PC?"

He had the decency to look sheepish.

"For five years? Since the ten-year reunion?"

"What makes you think that?"

"You couldn't have gotten your mail before eight o'clock this morning. You've known about this less than two hours. You didn't decide to turn into Mr. Wonderful and marry my sister in two hours. Your mind doesn't work that way," she added.

He lifted one broad shoulder and tilted her one of his sensual half smiles. "See. You know me well. If anyone can do this, it's you."

"You *are* a nerd," she said with the casual affection of their long-term friendship. "No one but a nerd would quietly obsess about his next high school reunion for five years. You are exactly the nerd everyone thought you were back then."

"A successful, rich nerd," he pointed out. "You said so yourself. Surely with my money and your flair for remodeling things, we can polish me up into something Mallory will find attractive."

"You don't have to do a thing," she said dryly. "Mallory did notice you made the cover of *Time* magazine."

"You didn't tell me that."

"I haven't seen you."

"True." His mouth puckered thoughtfully. "She noticed? She said something?"

"The last time I talked to her." Cindy compressed her lips and felt the ache build inside. *She'd* noticed. She'd called to congratulate him. He'd said an absentminded thanks and had to get off the phone. He didn't even remember.

She suppressed the urge to tell him how many times Mallory had quoted and questioned his net worth. Her sister had definitely wanted Cindy to confirm that the figures in the article were accurate.

Cindy was a little surprised Mallory hadn't called him, too.

"I don't want her to want me for the money," he said, reading her mind. "I want her to fall in love with me."

The vise around Cindy's heart tightened painfully. Life was so unfair.

"So will you help me, Cindy? You know more than anyone what makes Mallory tick. You know exactly the kind of men she's attracted to. And you know me," he added. "Will you teach me?"

She inwardly groaned. In the twenty-eight years of her life—every one of those years she'd known and idolized and loved him—she'd never been able to tell him no. It would probably take her another billion years to find the strength to say it. She couldn't now. Not even for this. Not even if it broke her heart and shredded every ounce of her pride and all of her dreams. "It ain't going to be easy," she said, struggling against the rasp in her throat to sound normal.

"Nothing worth doing is ever easy." He tagged an optimistic sigh at the end of what had almost become his motto. Then he smiled, took off his jacket and started rolling up his sleeves. "Guess I'd better go buy some cat litter. Do you have the soda?"

"Hey, you aren't getting off that easy."

He gave her that frowning, out-of-it, what-are-you-talking-about look.

"You think getting an oil stain off the floor of this garage is even close to a fair exchange for transforming you into a...hunk?"

He laughed in that sheepish little boy way of his.

"Not remotely," she said before he could protest. "You also have to help me..."

"What?"

She compressed her lips, her mind a total blank. "I'll think of plenty. We have four months before the reunion. Four months worth of various to-be-named favors *might* be a fair exchange. Believe me, it's going to take every second of that four months for my part of the task."

"I'm not that bad, am I?"

She crossed her arms and studied him head to toe. His square jaw clenched uneasily and he shifted self-consciously. His thick brown hair usually needed a trim and now was no exception. The sprig he'd left standing on end a moment ago still jutted from beneath a smooth strand of straight brown and another sprig fanned out from behind one ear. His impressive blue eyes looked myopic behind the heavy dark framed glasses. With his jacket gone, his white shirt sort of swallowed him, camouflaging his wonderful broad shoulders. His slacks were also a smidge too long and the hem fell in a fold over the tops of his battered running shoes. From time to time, she itched to do exactly what he wanted her to do now. But why now? Why for Mallory?

"You're not so bad that a wad of money and a lot of hard work won't fix you," she finally declared with only a tiny spark of malicious intent.

It missed its mark. "I'm not hopeless then," he deduced cheerfully.

No, he wasn't hopeless. She was. She was hopelessly in love with him. And it was time to get over him and get a life. She had four months to do it…if her slowly cracking heart didn't kill her before then.

"Come for lunch Saturday," he'd said when he'd finally left on Thursday after getting the oil stain off her garage floor. "We'll plan strategy."

Cindy looked down at the directions he'd written out for her and back up at the heavy black wrought-iron gates. The numbers matched. This had to be it. But this couldn't be the house he'd called to say he was moving to a few weeks ago. This wasn't a house, it was a...a...mansion?

She couldn't actually see the house so she didn't know if it was a mansion or not. But if the gates, the beautiful fountain just outside them and the grounds she glimpsed on the other side were any indication, it had to be something pretty spectacular.

But how did she get in?

By thinking about it, obviously. The gates slowly started to swing open. When she got even with the native stone columns holding the heavy gates, she saw a speaker phone imbedded there. Complete with camera, she noted as Parker's voice came through as clearly as if he was sitting beside her.

"Just follow the drive, Cindy," he said. "I'll be waiting for you out front."

A minute and a half later, Cindy saw him. Even the amazing glass and stone "castle" behind him couldn't hold her attention. Today he had on snug jeans and a bedraggled T-shirt. The jeans fit him nicely except they looked like he was expecting a flood. The shirt looked like a Salvation Army reject.

That's right, she told herself. Find every tiny thing wrong with him. Pick him apart, piece by piece. That was the only way to fix him. And each piece she picked, she was determined to turn over and examine for the slightest imperfection underneath. Aversion therapy. By the time she put him back together again for Mallory, she would see—really see—scads of stuff that would make him unappealing to her. They'd gloss over the top for Mallory, but Cindy would know it was just gloss. And she'd be over him.

"We have to take you shopping, PC," she said as soon as she stepped from the car. "You wear really pathetic clothes."

"That's the best you can do for a greeting?" His smile tilted.

"You asked for my expertise, not polite platitudes."

The slight lift of his shoulders said "Okay, you made your point." "What do you think?" He cast a glance at the house rising naturally from the landscape behind him. "Pretty impressive, isn't it?"

"Pretty impressive." He'd probably bought it to impress Mallory. It was the biggest house she'd ever seen in real life. Castle size and even castlelike in appearance with its native stone exterior. But masses of windows and glass modernized it. The rough golden beige slabs of stone curved around arches at the massive windows and pillared at the entryways. "Did you buy this with the reunion in mind?" The words stuck on the sore spot that had hovered in her chest since he'd walked into her garage and announced his intention to marry Mallory.

"No." It was small comfort that he looked at her as if she'd lost her mind.

She'd joined him on the stone walkway and he turned with her to admire the house.

"My accountant said it was a good investment and I needed one. I got it for less than it's worth since the sellers were anxious to get rid of it." He looked pleased with himself.

She pounced on the chink in his armor. Two chinks in his armor, she amended. He considered his house an investment, not a home and the Parker she'd always loved wouldn't be proud of taking advantage of someone else's misfortune. If she could focus on things like that—

"They built it ten years ago for a third of what it was appraised for," he added. "So we both ended up with a good deal."

Okay. Down to one chink. But it was a big one. Who would want a man who looked at his home only as an investment? Her sister, of course. She'd consider him very wise and savvy. "It can't hurt your chances with Mallory," she muttered.

His grin slipped. "That's not what I want, Cindy," he warned. His shoulders slumped as he led her through double doors of elegant etched glass and into a dramatic, vaulted foyer. Beyond them soaring columns divided the entry from a step down into a gigantic living room. Her own living room would have fit into the stone fireplace that lined one wall of the open room. The other side of the room was glass, taking full advantage of the view of wooded acreage beyond. There was absolutely nothing to block the view between where they were standing by the front door and the windows that seemed miles away. Absolutely nothing. No furniture. No pictures—well, except for a hand-painted mural on the wall behind them and a beautiful stairway that gracefully curved upward.

He led her through several empty rooms that echoed hollowly then through an opened door into a cozier room. "This is the master suite," he said. "Suite" was an understatement. It was a full apartment and the room they entered was the normal-size living room. Pointing out the bedroom, the bedroom-size closet, his smile tilted as he opened the door to a garage-size bathroom several cars would fit in. "Can you believe this?" His expression reminded her of the one he used to wear when he'd find a new gadget or gimmick or game for his "'puter" when he was first getting into them.

Mallory would love it. Dual everything. Mirrors and very expensive marble everywhere. It had a sauna and a steam room and a hot-tub-size whirlpool bath beside a wall of windows that overlooked the wooded property again.

"You could live in your bathroom—or the closet," Cindy commented as Parker led her back to the sitting room.

"I know." He grinned.

"This 'suite' is bigger than the house I'm working on."

He nodded and pointed to the kitchenette to one side of the room. It was separated from the sitting area by a countertop breakfast bar. "The kitchen's small."

"Oh, I'm sure you're suddenly going to take up cooking." Cindy could picture herself there, moving around in her robe, making coffee; maybe popcorn in the evening so they could cuddle in front of the wall-size TV and watch a movie. She didn't even have to close her eyes. She did now to block the vision. Fantasyland. If she was going to picture someone in his cute little black-and-white gleaming kitchen, it had to be Mallory.

He was explaining the set of stairs on the other side of his sitting room. They led down to an exercise room, he explained, and gave him private access to the basement beyond.

The master suite was furnished. The worn but comfortable furniture he'd had in his apartment looked out of place in the perfect room.

He'd put a pot of coffee on. Since he rarely drank it himself, he must have noticed at some point over the years that she was an addict. Her spirits lifted momentarily until she forced them to settle again. So he'd noticed *one* thing about her in their twenty-odd-year history. He should know her front to back, inside, outside and upside down. He finally remembered she drank coffee. So what? She kept a six-pack of cola on hand at all times—just in case he came around.

He grabbed a cola from the refrigerator after he'd placed a cup of coffee in front of her and settled beside her at the table set neatly in one end of the room.

They'd barely sat down when someone else breezed into the room. Cindy blinked twice, then rose from her chair. "Flo."

The familiar, round, little woman explained the coffee, Cindy thought with a flash of disappointment that evaporated quickly in her delight at seeing her very favorite neighbor again.

Flo set a plate of homemade cinnamon rolls in the middle of the small table and then took Cindy in her arms. "You're looking *fine,* child," she said as she folded Cindy against her plush frame.

"Oh, you, too, Flo. You, too. Where have you been? I thought you were still living with your daughter in Cleveland."

"I could have told you," Parker said from behind them.

"I was," Flo Kincaid answered Cindy's question, "until PC called me and talked me into coming to work for him." Flo held Cindy an arm's length away.

"I keep track of everyone from the old neighborhood," Parker said.

"You do?" Cindy asked blankly.

"That was the incentive for the new address book features in my most popular program." Parker launched into an explanation of the convenient way it worked in computerese.

Flo rolled her eyes and Cindy finally stopped him with an amused, "We don't have to understand your programs to make them work. That's why they're so popular, PC."

Flo laughed and for a few moments updates on her kids and various old neighbors dominated the conversation. "I'd better git so you two can plan your makeover strategy," Flo said finally.

The woman obviously knew what they were up to. "You think this is possible?" Cindy asked.

"If anyone believes he's Bachelor Of The Month material, it's you." Flo's look in Cindy's direction said Parker was probably the only person alive who didn't know how she felt about him. "I personally think you're fine the way you are," she added, placing her hands on her hips as she glared at him. "And I don't know why you'd want to bother about anyone who thinks you aren't." She blatantly didn't approve of Parker's plan. Or of Mallory, Cindy realized. But then Mallory had never been especially close to anyone in the old neighborhood. She hadn't been unfriendly; she'd just never taken the time to pay much attention to them.

"You still doing all that remodeling?" Flo changed the subject.

Cindy nodded proudly. "I'm totally on my own now, but yeah, I'm still remodeling."

"What do you mean, on your own?"

"I buy a house, remodel it start to finish, like I want. Then I sell it and buy another one and start the whole process over again. I rarely do odd jobs for other people now."

"You can do a house start to finish all by yourself?"

"There are a few things I have to hire help with," Cindy admitted. "I have a part-time helper—a kid in high school recommended by the same shop teacher who got me started."

"Mr. Havens?"

Cindy nodded. "I wait to do the heavier stuff until he's around, afternoons and Saturdays. It works really well."

"You're doing okay, then?"

"I'm doing okay," Cindy said semiproudly.

"I knew you would." Flo had been one of the few who hadn't thought Cindy was crazy when she started taking on small repair jobs for people around the old neighborhood. She'd taken woodworking her sophomore year in high school. Even though she and Parker had both been in the gifted program, "shop" had quickly become her most loved and best subject. She'd taken it every year after that. Gradually she'd acquired the reputation for being able to fix someone's door if it didn't close right or repair trim around a window. Small projects had evolved into bigger ones, like replacing a bathroom floor because someone had let the water leak under the sink go on too long.

Flo had been the first paying customer because she'd insisted and Cindy had been "on the job" ever since. She'd been the most affordable Ms. Fix It around. She'd purchased and learned to use various tools for each project as she went along.

"I'd probably still be doing the same old small odd jobs for everyone if the old neighborhood was still there," she admitted.

"You were never fond of change, were you," Flo sympathized.

"I guess not."

"You must be making a good living now," Parker commented from his vast store of knowledge on the subject. He forked the last bite of the cinnamon roll Flo had put on his plate into his mouth.

"I wish." She punctuated the comment with a sigh. "This last house is going to be a tough sell, I'm afraid. I may be back to doing odd jobs."

"It looked great." Parker frowned. He'd seen the "before" when she bought it six months ago; she'd shown him the "after" the other day when he'd gotten the oil spot out of the garage floor. "Why do you think I'm so confident you can transform me," he added.

"Fortunately," Cindy said wryly, "no one is going to put a halfway house right down the street from you."

Flo and Parker both frowned.

"You know, one of those places where they put kids after they've been in juvenile hall but before they let them go back to whatever home they originally had? It kind of annihilates property values for a little while until people see how it's going to affect the area."

"It'll be okay." Flo patted her hand.

"I know it will eventually." In the meantime, Cindy would have to wait for a buyer as confident in the area's potential as she was.

"You think people will expect crime in the area to rise?" Parker asked.

She told him what her usual real estate saleswoman had told her. "People will just be nervous of moving to or investing in the neighborhood for a while. Till they see what happens."

"So selling may take a while," Flo said, understanding.

"Or I'll have to cut my profit to nothing and settle for a price to cover what I have invested," Cindy agreed. "But enough of my problems. That's not—"

"I don't understand," Flo broke in.

"She uses her profits from one house to buy another and fix it up."

"And I live in the house while I'm working on it. That's the only way I've kept my head above water so far. It keeps my living expenses to a minimum," Cindy explained patiently.

"So you won't have anywhere to live when you sell this one." Flo asked, frowning.

"I won't have any profits. No profits, no house to buy to work on *or* to live in," Cindy told her. "It's like when Parker was first starting—well, kinda. He made money hand over fist from the very beginning, but don't you remember when he was sweating his monthly expenses and putting every cent of profit back into the business?"

Flo's blank look suddenly cleared. "Oh. I see."

Cindy exchanged a glance with Parker. "This was the house I hoped would get me ahead. I had a profit margin figured in that would allow me to start paying myself a monthly salary," she admitted, adding with exasperation. "And I planned to buy my next house in the same neighborhood. It is…was," she corrected, "becoming really nice. Stable. The people there have made great strides, cleaning it up, running out some of the bad elements. And with all the nice big old houses and it sort of overlooks downtown…" She let the rest of the comment remain unsaid.

"The potential is good," Parker offered.

Cindy nodded. "Was," she felt obligated to tack on.

"So the halfway house complicates things for you," Flo analyzed.

"Temporarily. It's just going to slow me down."

"Maybe you should put your name in to remodel the halfway house."

Cindy had always loved Flo. They thought the same way. "I did." She grimaced. "They'd already hired a big name contractor."

"You can come to work for me," Parker offered for the hundredth time. He'd been trying to get her to work for him at PC, Inc., since he'd started it. Said she'd be the best personal assistant he could find.

"You know I would hate working in an office," she gave him her standard reply, though her reasons for turning him down had just gotten stronger. *I couldn't stand seeing you every day and knowing there was never a hope of you loving me,* she added to herself. *And I'd never get over you.*

"You know the offer's good if you need something temporary to get you through."

"He just wants you at his beck and call while you're trying to perform this miracle," Flo warned, laughing. "He tried the same thing with me. Tried to get me to move into the staff apartment."

It was Cindy's turn to look blank.

"Oh. You haven't seen the whole house?"

Cindy shook her head.

"Just wait," Flo cautioned. "You ought to see me trying to figure out when and where to serve his meals."

"Maybe moving in would be easier," Cindy suggested.

"I'm close enough," Flo laughed. "I have the caretaker's cottage out back," Flo bragged. "I can see when his lights come on in here. I come up and serve his dinner—usually in here—then go back to my own little place, though cottage doesn't do it justice. It's the nicest house I've ever had," she said, her eyes alight with pride. "Big enough to enjoy my kids and grandkids without sending out search parties to look for them."

"That's a shot at this house," Parker explained to Cindy in case she hadn't caught it.

"I noticed." Cindy was enjoying the old I-can-give-as-good-as-I-get atmosphere of the old neighborhood.

"This is a warehouse," Flo said. "Don't let him kid you. You just don't notice because you don't leave this little suite of rooms." She aimed the statement at him. She indicated his rooms with an expansive gesture. "Or he doesn't leave the office," she added to Cindy. "He's becoming a workaholic."

Workaholic, Cindy noted at the top of her pad. She was enjoying the warmth and companionship of this free-for-all way too much. It was time to get it back on track. "I'm making a list of things we need to tackle if we're going to do this magical transformation," she explained when Parker asked what she was doing. "Mallory's the type who needs intensive care and attention," she added dryly. "You can't stay a workaholic if you expect to hold her interest. What do you think did in her first marriage?"

Parker straightened in his chair. "That's exactly the kind of stuff I need to learn, isn't it?"

"You're going to have to turn yourself into Mallory's lapdog," Flo muttered under her breath. "Cindy's only agreed to turn you into Prince Charming."

Cindy laughed at Flo's succinct summary of the whole situation and instantly felt traitorous. "Prince Charming's enough of a challenge, don't you think," she managed to say brightly.

"More than enough." Flo returned, rising to her feet and excusing herself to get back to work.

"That's enough," Parker echoed with a contented sigh. "Prince Charming—" he preened "—I think I can handle that."

CHAPTER TWO

CINDY'S first step on any project was making a list.
This one she titled: Parker Project.

With little input from him, Cindy's list grew. Every
item she added, she expected him to defend himself,
as she would if someone decided to take her apart,
piece by piece. He sat instead, looking fascinated
while she squirmed. At last, the column of items she'd
written seemed complete.

"Can you think of anything else?" she asked him,
turning the pad so he could look her list over.

It wasn't as long as Cindy had anticipated and
some of the items would be simple.

"If I knew what I needed to change, I wouldn't
need help from you, would I," he teased, then
scowled as he looked at it.

"What?"

He pointed to the first item on the list.

Workaholic? He hadn't gotten past the first item?

"What can I do about that?" he asked as if the
problem was something he couldn't possibly help or
change.

"Quit working around the clock," she said. "Don't
worry," she added at his blank look. "I'll remind you
several times between now and the reunion."

"And who, do you suggest, will do my work?"

"You. It would help, PC, if when you aren't working, you could actually pay attention to other things.
Like the person you're with," she added as an ex-

ample. "You could occasionally think of your friends. You just can't ignore people for months on end." She grinned to salvage her pride for bringing it up.

His scowl deepened.

"Like me," she tried again. "We're supposed to be friends, but I often don't hear from you for months. I didn't even know your new address." She gestured at their surroundings.

"My phone number didn't change. You can call me any time."

She ignored him. "Friends—and especially someone you might want to marry," she clarified so he wouldn't realize it was personal, "tend to want to know they're important to you, that you think of them from time to time. They want to know what's going on in your life."

"You never seem to mind," he pointed out.

Cindy bit back the words she wanted to say. Instead she took a deep breath. "I know you've been busy. But I don't count in this discussion," she said calmly. "You didn't say you wanted to marry me. Someone you expect to marry will want your attention." Her lips twisted on the words as if she was eating a sour pickle.

But he was still on the last subject. "I consider you my closest friend," he said.

"But I never know on a regular basis what's going on with you." She let him draw her in. "Why didn't you tell me Flo was working for you?" she asked. "Or invite me over to see your house after you moved?"

"She just started since I last saw..." He let the words trail off.

"And that's been?"

"Maybe two months," he said sheepishly after mulling it over.

"Six weeks," she told him.

"You can call me anytime," he told her again.

"I know," she agreed. "But until you decide to call me, your head is so far in the clouds it's a waste of time trying to find out what's going on with you. You're working whether you're at work or not."

"I've been there when you needed me," he said half defensively.

"Yes," she admitted. Since junior high, he'd listened to every problem, helped her study for tests, been there in hundreds of ways. The only thing she hadn't been able to talk to him about was boys, probably because he'd always been the only one on her mind. Three years ago, when she'd been trying to get up the nerve to buy her first house, he'd listened for hours on end. He'd made a mathematical chart only a genius could figure out to prove she could afford to do what she wanted. He'd given advice when needed and when asked. But day to day, if she didn't have a problem or he didn't have something specific he wanted to talk to her about, he was zoned out. "You've always been there when I needed you, PC."

"That's another thing," he said, raising one finger. "Do you think I should insist my old classmates call me Parker? Doesn't that sound more...more..."

"Like someone Mallory would marry," she finished for him.

"More adult." He frowned at her as if he wanted to argue with the way she'd said it. "Does PC sound too much like a childish nickname?"

Too much like who you were? Not like who you

want to be. "It's you, PC." She smiled. "Parker Chaney. Politically Correct. Personal Computer expert. It's even your company name," she added.

"It seemed right at the time." He shrugged.

"You could encourage everyone at the reunion to call you Chaney, like they did throughout the *Times* article."

"They called me PC," he reminded her.

"Just in the first paragraph," she said, quoting, "'Even the name Parker Chaney's friends and close associates call him is synonymous with the industry his company dominates. Personal Computers. No one who owns or touches one has been untouched by PC, Inc. The company's faster, smarter and better innovations barrage the technological market on an almost daily basis.'"

"You memorized it?" His sky-blue eyes lit.

"I read it enough times to remember it," she said, lifting one shoulder.

His crooked grin matched the way hers felt. "I'm *not* an especially thoughtful friend, am I?" He reached across the table to cover her hand with his. Bracing herself for the normal electrical charge she got at his touch, she was pleasantly surprised when it didn't happen. She'd managed to numb herself, she thought triumphantly. Or maybe the message that there was no longer any hope had gotten through to her brain and her body was shutting down her reactions to him in acceptance.

He looked dazed, as startled as she'd ever seen him. She squirmed self-consciously. Maybe her body hadn't reacted, but had her expression given something away?

He lifted his hand, gingerly rubbing his palm, then

laced his fingers together and rested his hands carefully on his side of the table.

"Whatever is happening with you, whatever you're doing, you've always been a three-in-the-morning friend," she told him. "That means a lot to me."

He was scowling again. "And what, exactly, is a three-in-the-morning friend?"

"Don't you remember my dad talking about that when we were young?" Since his own father had taken off when Parker was small, he'd hung around with her and her dad a lot.

Parker shook his head.

"It isn't necessarily the people you see every day, or the person you *think* you'd call," she explained. "It's someone you wouldn't hesitate to contact anytime—day or night—if you needed help. Even at three in the morning. For any kind of help. You've always been that kind of friend for me, PC. I want you to know how much I appreciate it."

"You make it sound...past tense." He looked downright uneasy with the thought. "That isn't going to—"

"I was thinking about it the other day...after you asked me to help you," she interrupted. "With Mallory?"

His eyes were the color of a cloudy day now.

"If...when," she corrected, "you marry Mallory, it will change." She stopped him with a raised hand as he opened his mouth to protest. "We'll still be friends. I know I'll be able to come to you with almost anything."

"We'd be family then." His voice emphasized the words determinedly.

"You'll be my brother-in-law. Wouldn't it seem strange to call you for help instead of my sister?"

"You'd be calling both of us."

"I love Mallory but I could never call her with my problems at three o'clock in the morning," she said quietly.

"But you guys are close." He looked guilty.

That wasn't Cindy's intent. "It doesn't matter," she said. "I love Mallory dearly, but she's not a call-me-with-your-problems-at-three-in-the-morning type person. But it will be fun having someone I feel so close to as a brother-in-law. What a change of pace!" She managed a short laugh. "A brother-in-law I will actually know."

"Nothing will change," he assured her. Or maybe he was reassuring himself. Then he sat up straighter, thumping the list that was still in front of him. "Well, I guess some things better change or all this is a pipe dream."

She grinned at him, her very best friend as long as she could remember. "I'm not losing a friend, I'm gaining family." She'd missed having 'family' since her parents' death in a freak weather accident when she was fifteen years old. "Who would have guessed," she forced a lighthearted tone into her voice, "that I would ever know someone as important as you, let alone be related. I guess it's kind of unrealistic of me to expect to hear from you more. I do keep track, though," she added. "I saw the interview on CNN last month."

"You did?"

She nodded. "You were great."

"I sounded like a total egghead." He was still studying her with that bemused and confused look.

"You sounded very impressive, PC," she said. "You managed to make the interviewer laugh a couple of times. I was proud of you."

"I was proud of me, too," he admitted, quieter than he'd been. "I am getting better at that sort of thing."

"Do you have any choice with all the practice you're getting?"

"Nah, I guess not."

Cindy got irritated with herself. She was sounding as if she were the charter member of his Admiration Society again. She stiffened her spine and returned to their original subject. "You'll never be my brother-in-law if you don't marry Mallory." She somehow managed to keep the bittersweet pain out of her voice as she pointed to the list. "We'd better get busy with the stuff you aren't so good at."

His smile faded and he turned his attention to the second item. "Clothes?"

"We'll go through your closet in a little while," Cindy suggested.

Parker pointed to the next item and scowled. "What's wrong with my hair?"

Cindy pulled the list over and added Habit of Scowling to the bottom of it. "You need a decent haircut, PC. You need something with a little style. We'll get you an appointment with someone really good. I know a stylist downtown who'd be perfect…has great taste and a good eye," she raved enthusiastically.

Parker looked skeptical. "The guy does your hair?"

Cindy knew him too well to think he was insulting

her; he must be trying to figure out how she knew him. "He bought my last house," she explained.

"A definite sign of great taste." Parker grinned and moved on, showing exactly how unimportant he thought his hairstyle was, despite his initial response.

"We should check into getting you contacts," she said as his finger tapped at the next word: Glasses. It had a question mark beside it. "Or if you don't want contacts, surely your eye doctor has more fashionable frames than those."

"What's wrong with these?"

"Nothing if you don't mind looking like you bought cheap magnifying eyeglasses at the discount store."

Parker looked up at her, flushing, then down at the nail he'd been flicking against the list.

"You don't, PC," Cindy protested. "Tell me you didn't buy those glasses off a display rack in some drugstore."

"They work." He met her gaze. "My eyes aren't that bad. I broke my prescription glasses a couple of years ago when I was out of town and bought some like this to get me through the emergency. I discovered I didn't really need much, just something when I sit staring at a computer screen all day."

"You've worn glasses all your life, Parker Chaney."

"Mom used to make me go to the eye doctor at least once a year," he said. "But when mine broke and I didn't have time..."

"In how many years?"

"Five, maybe six," he muttered.

Cindy pointed to the pad in front of him. "Put that on the list, PC. Top of the list. First thing Monday morning. You have to get an appointment with an optometrist." She rolled her eyes. "And I wondered why you were getting such geeky glasses the past few years. I couldn't imagine that your doctor didn't have more fashionable ones."

"But you think I should get contacts," he pointed out.

"If you can wear them," she said. "You have beautiful blue eyes, PC. You should let—"

"You think so?" he interrupted. The beautiful blue eyes narrowed. His voice lowered. "You think I have beautiful eyes?"

If she didn't know better, she'd think he was flirting. She willed herself not to flush but wasn't certain she was successful. "I'm guessing," she said sarcastically. "It's hard to tell behind those things."

"Should I get colored lenses?"

"Why mess up such an interesting shade?"

He laughed and she realized she'd fallen into his trap. Okay, she'd admitted she thought his eyes were beautiful. They were a very normal blue, except they were flecked with gray. It made them seem the color of the sky on a beautiful day. Studying his gorgeous eyes was exactly the kind of habit she had to break. She looked away.

He finished perusing the list as Flo stuck her head in the door to check on them. "How's it coming?"

"What do you think?" Cindy invited her in to look over the items they'd come up with.

Flo read over his shoulder, looking as skeptical about some of it as Cindy felt. "You'd better do something about his manners, too."

Parker looked indignant.

"I don't mean manner manners," she said before

he could protest. "I mean...you know." She waved toward Cindy. "The way he moves."

"You mean mannerisms," Cindy said, frowning herself.

"Mannerisms," Flo agreed. "It won't be as hard as it sounds," she added a promise for Parker. "He's very graceful when he's relaxed or not being self-conscious. You've seen him dance," she added as Cindy nodded. "Like a stick figure. Stick legs."

"You think we can do something about that," Cindy wondered aloud, adding Mannerisms to the list.

"He isn't that bad. Just self-conscious—like he'll be if all this comes off—he'll get stiff and awkward. You'll just have to figure out some way to make him relax. Take him dancing. Practice until he's comfortable." Flo danced around the table, holding an imaginary partner. "But not just dancing," she warned. "You'll have to take on all those things that make people think he's a computer geek. Like walking across a room with his shoulders scrunched when he's concentrating. Or squinting continually," she pointed out as he did it again.

Cindy tapped the end of her pen at Scowling on the list. "It might help if he got the proper glasses," she stated.

"You need to practice all of this on Cindy." Flo snapped her fingers as if the idea had just struck her. But her expression was too smug.

Cindy felt a knot grow in the pit of her stomach. That's all she needed, someone playing matchmaker while she was trying to fix him up for Mallory.

"Practice on Cindy," Flo reiterated. "Call her. Take her out. Wine and dine her. Go dancing."

"Lousy idea," Cindy protested.

"Practice makes perfect." Flo ignored her and directed the remark at Parker.

"It's brilliant," he said, sprawling back in his chair, folding his arms over his chest. His feet tangled with hers under the table.

She shifted uncomfortably and straightened the pad as if it were a stack of papers. "It's silly. You've been comfortable with me forever," she said. "So how is that going to help you with Mallory?"

Parker fixed her with those intent eyes. "I'll—" he searched for a word "—woo you. It would make me plenty uncomfortable and awkward. It will be great practice."

"It would make us both 'plenty uncomfortable and awkward.' And what good would it do? I'm not at all like Mallory."

He compressed his lips, studying her. "But you know what *you* like. What one woman likes in a man can't be that much different from another."

"Sure. That's why Mallory's been married twice and I don't even have a boyfriend. See? We don't think alike. Besides, how am I supposed to react to being 'wooed'?"

"What do you mean?"

"Am I supposed to playact, too? Play like I'm falling in love with you," she added when he scrunched his face into an incomprehensible mess.

"Just tell me what I do wrong and what I do right." He spread his hands as if it made all the sense in the world. "That's all you'd have to do. I learn best from experience."

She continued to shake her head.

He covered her hand with one of his, letting the corners of his mouth turn up slowly. "If you're concerned that I'll get some weird, romantic notion..." He let the statement finish itself.

He'd said it in his most sincere, totally clueless way. It was the remark of the true Parker she knew and loved—the Parker Chaney she had to *quit* loving. And probably the best way to do that was to turn him into exactly what he wanted to be: someone Mallory would love. "Don't worry, PC," she said softly, disengaging her hand from his. "I'm not concerned about anything like that."

"You don't trust me."

"What does trust have to do with anything?" It wasn't *him* she didn't trust. It was herself. "But you can't experiment with people like you do one of your computer programs."

"You're right, Cindy." Flo met Cindy's gaze across the top of Parker's head. "It was a lousy idea. I take it back," she said, an apology in her eyes.

Cindy sighed and picked up her pen. "Now, shouldn't we figure out how to deal with all of this realistically if we want to rescue you from geekdom?"

"I've done rather well with it," he said, lifting his straight, perfect nose and showing an arrogance Cindy had seen more and more often the past couple of years. His success hadn't gone to his head exactly, but he had slowly changed, gained an inner confidence that had been missing when he was younger. He no longer slinked into a room and lurked on the fringes as he had when faced with a crowd back in high school.

Just last week, she'd seen a clip of him on the nightly business news on TV. Some company had just signed a contract with his company and the cameras were there, witnessing the agreement. There had been a presence, a proud swagger, a tall assurance in the way he'd held his shoulders as the camera caught him shaking hands with that company's CEO. She'd noted his easy grace at the time and felt proud for him. Other people must have seen him the same way because stock in PC, Inc. soared more than four points the next day. But business was different. Social situations tied him in knots.

"You're right. You've done extremely well," Cindy told him primly, laying the pen back down with a snap. "Anyone who isn't impressed with who and what you are can just go to hell. Who cares what anyone thinks."

"Except…" He looked confused.

"Mallory?" Winning the point didn't give Cindy a bit of satisfaction. Poor Parker. And poor Mallory if she didn't appreciate what she was getting, Cindy decided.

"She does like heads to turn when she makes an appearance on the arm of some man," he stated after a moment. The analytical, problem-solving, step-back-and-view-things-from-a-distance side of him had returned.

"She always did *that* by herself," Flo said, a touch too wryly.

"But she expects her attachments to be impressive, too."

Cindy and Flo looked at Parker with amazement. He'd used the word "attachment." Obviously he was aware that Mallory saw whatever man she was with as another of her accessories. He was coming along.

"Speaking of impressing people. Something else you should think about doing," Cindy suggested.

"What?"

"You should consider hosting one of the reunion events here," she told him. The idea had struck when she'd first stepped into his new foyer, though she'd been in too much shock to voice it then. "What better chance to impress everyone?" Including Mallory, she almost heard Parker think as he noted it with a raised eyebrow.

"You don't think being on the *Times* cover is enough to impress anyone?"

"Now you're gloating."

"He does take extra pleasure out of all his success, doesn't he," Flo teased.

"I'll admit. I look forward to observing a few people's reactions."

Cindy chuckled. "Bill Baxter, for one?" He'd been the star running back on the high school football team. He'd dated Mallory throughout their senior year.

"Baxter's a start." Parker leaned forward, propping his elbows on the table as he twisted the pen he held between both hands. "What kind of event did you have in mind?"

"A cocktail party maybe? The committee's tentative schedule said a 'Get Together' on Friday evening? But it wasn't specific. Since nothing was spelled out, I'll bet they haven't finalized anything yet. If you called the committee and volunteered to have their Get Together here—kind of a renew-old-acquaintances informal cocktail party—I'll bet they'd jump on it."

He nodded thoughtfully. "That sounds logical."

"And *that* phrase you should strike from your vocabulary,'' Flo said, dishing another warm roll onto each of their plates.

"That sounds logical?"

"Yeah." Cindy shared another understanding smile with Flo. "Strange as it may seem, PC, not everyone in the world functions strictly on logic," she added. "Mallory will not be impressed when you ask her to marry you by detailing the logic behind it. You might want to mention feelings or emotion or something similar."

He laughed. Nothing perked him up like the mention of Mallory.

"She'll see plenty of logic on her own," Cindy muttered under her breath. *Darn him. And darn me for caring.*

Flo chuckled. "I gotta get back to work. Sounds like you guys are doing just fine." She picked up the pan with the rest of the rolls. "It's good to see you again, Cindy. I'm glad we'll be doing it a lot more often."

"Thanks, Flo. Me, too."

Flo gave a thumbs-up on her way out.

"Why do I get the feeling I've invited the two of you to gang up on me," Parker asked as she closed the door behind her.

"It's your imagination." Cindy reviewed their list again. She didn't need to worry about still being in love with him when all this was over. If they accomplished everything on here, he'd be a totally different man. Someone she wouldn't recognize, let alone love. That was good, wasn't it?

Was it the idea of him changing that made her feel so irritable and sad? Or was it that she was making him over for Mallory?

Cindy looked around her at the luxurious apartment he and Flo had christened the master suite. "I was serious, PC," she said. "You really don't need to do anything except bring everyone here. You'll have the undivided attention of every unmarried female in your class."

"I was serious, too," he replied as passionately as she'd ever heard him. "I don't want anyone who's only attracted to all this."

Not even Mallory? She clamped her mouth closed over the next question she wanted to ask. How would they know *what* Mallory would be interested in. Because she would be interested.

Cindy closed her eyes momentarily. She couldn't protect him from Mallory; she couldn't even protect him from himself. She could only do her very best for him and let her feelings for him go. They were hopeless. She'd known it as long as she could remember. It was time to start thinking of him as the brother-in-law he wanted to be.

"Then don't worry. By the time we're through with you, she'll be dazzled by just you." She forced a smile. "So where do you want to start?"

"First things first. Might as well begin at the beginning." He leaned closer, eager to do whatever he was required. He grimaced and tapped at the word topping the list: Workaholic.

"You'll have to do that one yourself," she reminded him, adding, "but if it makes you feel better, I'll remind you from time to time."

"It's surely a matter of concentration," he said, causing her to shake her head. That's what got him into trouble in the first place—concentrating too hard.

He scanned the list again from top to bottom. "Is there anything *right* with me?" he asked ruefully.

Her heart compressed in her chest. *There is so much* right *with you, Parker Michael Chaney!* She loved his honesty. His intensity. His dedication and determination. His genuine caring. His way of making whatever he wanted to happen happen. She released a painfully silent sigh. "The problem has always been perceptions," she said. "*Their* perceptions," she clarified. "Your former classmates. The problem has never been with you."

"But now, fifteen years later, I have an opportunity to make a new first impression," he said, pleased with the thought.

"Exactly."

"I can't tell you how badly I want to do that." He squared his shoulders. "So I guess it's logical...appropriate," he amended, "to start on this one." He underlined the second with his finger. "Clothes." He glanced up expectantly.

"Then I guess we should adjourn to your closet."

CHAPTER THREE

His closet was the size of her bedroom. Beside it there was another one the same size. Out of curiosity, Cindy opened that door as Parker opened the one he'd indicated was his. She wasn't surprised to see boxes stacked inside the second one. Boxes, computer keyboards, various pieces and parts of computers. In this huge house, there had to be another place to store those kinds of things.

With an overwhelmed sigh, she closed the second door.

"What?" Parker asked. "What's wrong?" He was standing just inside the door he had opened.

"You'll have to clear all that stuff out for Mallory," she warned.

A can't-wait-for-Christmas expression spread across his face as the implication of her statement sank in. "I can handle that," he said and she could almost see the visions of sugarplums dancing in his head.

"PC..."

He looked at her, ready to do whatever she said.

"That's the first thing we have to change," she said, suddenly irritated beyond belief with him.

"What?"

"You have to get rid of that eager-to-please, can't-wait-for-you-to-walk-all-over-me attitude. Mallory's going to swallow you up for breakfast and throw you away."

43

He looked hurt.

"Every feeling you have can't show," she softened her tone a bit.

"Make up your mind," he said. "A minute ago you were telling me I had to express feelings, not logic."

"I said you had to *have* feelings. I didn't say you should wear them on your sleeve. For some reason, women like to be kept guessing just a tiny bit. You have to at least play a little hard to get." Shoot, maybe that was why *she* liked him. He'd kept her guessing and wishing and hoping for years. And how much harder to get could you be than madly, blindly in love with someone else?

"You can't be so...so...eager," she told him. "Lesson one—when Mallory says something, don't jump as if her tiniest wish is your command."

"So you don't want me to clean out the closet?"

This time her sigh was frustrated because she couldn't decide if she wanted to hit him or hug him. "Yes. Clean out the closet. But she doesn't have to know you did it for her. Shoot, don't do it for her. Do it for yourself! We're going to buy you a whole new wardrobe. Maybe you'll be using some of the space by the time this reunion comes around. Surely in this huge house you have somewhere to keep your old modems and stuff besides your bedroom." She waved vaguely at the door she'd shut.

His expression cleared some, but there were still tiny frown lines between his eyebrows. Cindy resisted the urge to smooth it away. "Don't take everything so literally," she snapped. "That's another problem. You take everything anyone says as gospel. People do say one thing and mean something else."

The frown deepened. "What do you mean?"

"I mean...for example, when I said you'd have to clean out the closet, I was talking to you, but I was mostly thinking out loud. In fact, it's kind of silly to clean it out until you know where all this is going to lead. Mallory may not be interested. Shoot, by the time she gets here, she may be married again." She wanted to slap the startled look off his face.

"You think that's a possibility?"

"I think," she measured her response, "you shouldn't worry. If she's madly in love with someone else and already married again, do you really want her?"

She couldn't bear to see the answer he might have in his eyes and turned away. "Never mind. She would have told me if she was thinking of getting married again." She changed the subject quickly and promised herself that whatever she felt, she would not make snide remarks about Mallory again. She *was* her sister. Cindy did love her, even though she didn't understand her. And she had to admit, she'd always been jealous of Parker's reaction to Mallory. "It's your house, and until something changes, you *shouldn't* clean out the closet if you want that stuff there."

"It is convenient," he said.

"Then don't clean it out." She shook her head to clear the confusion he created every time she had one of these literal/euphemistic conversations with him. "If it gets to the point where Mallory is considering settling in here, I'm sure she'll figure out some way to get you to move those things out herself."

Cindy pushed past him and looked at the meager number of clothes he had hanging in his own closet.

It held maybe ten suits, at least one of them dating back as far as high school—she recognized it from his and Mallory's graduation. There was a line of white shirts and a hanger with neckties hung haphazardly over it. His clothes took up maybe two feet of the clothing rods that ran at least thirty feet on three sides of the room. The walls were lined with cedar. Built-in drawers and cabinets were interspersed between the rods and shelving of various heights and sizes. Four pairs of sneakers in various stages of disintegration perched neatly on a long low shelf obviously meant for the purpose. He had sweaters and casual knit shirts folded neatly on one stretch of shelves.

Only two suits survived her scrutiny. "What's wrong with that one?" Parker asked at one point.

"Besides the fact that it's threadbare?" She reclaimed the suit he looked reluctant to part with.

"That's my TV suit," he protested.

"Why? Because someone told you to wear somber black when you're being interviewed?"

"And it's comfortable," he said, confirming her guess. "It's the most comfortable suit I have."

"Then we'll have to keep comfort in mind when we shop." She hauled a stack of clothes into the outer bedroom. "We can give these to the Salvation Army," she said. "Maybe you could have Flo take care of that?"

He pulled a miniature notepad from his back pocket, complete with a small pen attached by a little loop. "Let me make a note," he said, doing it as he spoke.

"It's a good thing money is no object," she said

as she brushed past him with another load of stuff she'd taken from one of the shelves.

One by one, she went through the casual shirts, dividing them into two stacks: a giveaway and one neatly folded one to go back onto the shelves.

"That one's almost new," he protested as she tossed one toward the charity pile.

Placing one hand on her hip, she asked, "What size do you wear, PC?"

He frowned as if it were a tough question.

She stepped around the side of the huge bed and held the shirt in question up to him. "Without looking, I can see this isn't your size." She pressed the shoulder seams against him. They hit midway down his arms. Then she checked the label. "It's a double X," she added dryly. "You've filled out a lot since high school, but not that much." She started to toss it toward the discard stack.

Parker caught it. "I like this shirt."

"Then we'll buy another like it. Or similar," she said, taking it out of his grasp.

His hand folded around hers as she started to pitch it again. The jolt of energy that had been missing when he'd touched her earlier came full force. He was eight inches away, staring her down. The only thing between them was their entwined fists and the wadded yellow shirt, hanging like a brightly colored tent.

At some point, his store-bought glasses had been pushed to the top of his head and his semishaggy haircut stood in random spikes around them. His bright blue eyes challenged her. His jaw firmed, rippling a muscle and drawing her attention. He set his mouth.

"You have such nice, broad shoulders, PC," she

heard herself say in a voice that sounded breathless to her ears. "Why do you want to drape them in a tent so no one can admire them?" The second part sounded almost natural, she thought. A little forced, but with a tinge of her normal sarcasm.

As she watched, he let a small slash of his straight white teeth show between very mesmerizing parted lips. What-would-it-be-like-if-he-kissed-me thoughts filled her mind and she groaned inwardly. Darn him. Darn him for touching her. Darn him for wanting Mallory. Darn her for agreeing to help him.

He studied her face with the same intensity he'd study some string of computer language he was determined to make do some magical computer thing. His stubborn look evolved to one of bewilderment and he tentatively touched her cheek.

Cindy shrugged away from him. "Keep it. If it's that important, keep it," she said, avoiding his stare. She could almost see his mind tick as he continued to study her. Darn him! Had he realized how much she wanted him to kiss her? After all this time, had he finally noticed? She wanted to cry. She prayed she was wrong because her pride couldn't take it if he started pitying her.

For the next twenty minutes, she worked her way through the rest of his things and avoided looking at him. By the time she was finished, she had her emotions well in hand.

She noticed at some point, without another word, Parker had put the shirt they'd struggled over in the giveaway pile.

"You think I have nice shoulders," he said, finally breaking his silence.

"Don't you?" she managed to ask nonchalantly,

as if they were talking about the weather. "I suspect when you added the workout facilities for your employees in the new building, you started using them yourself."

He grinned. "You're the first person who noticed."

"Maybe it's because you insist on wearing clothes that don't fit," she suggested.

"We're going shopping now? This afternoon?"

"Unless you have other plans," she agreed.

"Then you think I can do this transformation thing," he asked with a hint of the wonder she found so endearing.

"Listen," she said semigruffly, "if you'll notice the list, it's all—or almost all," she amended, "the topping. The icing on the cake. You've always been good-looking. You just don't capitalize on it. We're going to polish. That's all. And the sooner we get started, the better."

He looked skeptical. "If you say so."

"I say so, PC." Her sudden laugh startled him. "And then 'PC' will stand for one more thing," she added.

"Oh? What?" He scowled.

"Prince Charming, PC. You'll be PC for Prince Charming."

His car was the one thing he'd splurged on since he started making "real" money...well, until the new castlelike house, Cindy amended. But that didn't count, she decided, glancing back to see it disappear behind the trees and the curve in the driveway. He considered the house an investment, not a splurge. Not a home.

The tour he'd taken her on after they'd gone

through his clothes had lasted almost two hours—and they hadn't dawdled. It was a house five families could live in without running into each other. She'd lost count at seven bedrooms, tucked here, there and everywhere. Three kitchens.

Her favorite room—or one of her favorites—had been the empty music room. The step up into the room imitated a gigantic piano keyboard designed with inlaid, exotic, imported wood. She'd always wanted to learn to play the piano, she thought wistfully, not that Parker had one. Just a replica on a keyboard in the floor.

She'd also loved what he'd christened the 'tree house.' A completely glass-walled, circular room, it jutted out over the sloping wooded landscape. You got there via a glassed-in walkway from the living room. It was actually furnished since it had built-in seating and plush cushions all the way around and he obviously used it. The morning paper had still been scattered over the low circular table in the middle. All the windows opened, he'd explained and she could feel the peace of sitting there on a warm spring day just by being in the room.

Parker zipped his fancy BMW through the wide-open gates and apologized that it wasn't warm enough to put the convertible top of the two-seater down.

When he'd bought the car several years ago, Cindy hadn't thought a thing about it. Now, she wondered whether her sister's possible reaction to the car explained Parker's "splurge." Mal had always *oohed* and *aahed* over *anyone* who drove a Beamer. If he'd obsessed for five years over a reunion, why wouldn't he buy a specific car for the same reason.

But Mallory had owned two Beamers herself now,

courtesy of husband number two. She might not be as enthusiastic about them.

Cindy considered warning him, then decided not to think about it at all. She let her head fall back against the soft leather and shut her eyes, savoring the feel of the sun blazing through the window, warming her skin. Winter had seemed endless this year. The late February hints of spring were enough to lift her spirits, despite all the depressing stuff going on in her life. Spring. New life. New directions.

Parker turned the radio up and a golden oldie, far older than either of them, swirled around her. For a few minutes he just drove. And hummed off-key. "Where to," he finally called over the music.

She named the closest mall and hoped it wasn't too busy. She hated Saturdays at any mall.

She also hated shopping with Parker.

No wonder the man looked like a charity ward reject most of the time, she thought halfway through their fourth argument in their second store.

"Why did you like that one suit you didn't want me to give away?" Cindy asked, trying a new tactic. They hadn't bought one thing yet as Parker insisted he didn't need to try anything on.

He frowned. "It was comfortable?"

Cindy waited for him to come to the obvious conclusion. When he didn't, she sighed wearily. "Wouldn't you like *all* your clothes to be comfortable, PC," she said as if he were a little boy.

"Trying them on is not going to make them comfortable," he declared, mystified by the connection.

"You don't *buy* anything that isn't comfortable," she explained sweetly. "And you can't find that out if you don't try them on."

The light dawned. On her, too. No wonder he'd struggled to keep the shirt that was three sizes too big. It was comfortable.

It also explained the running shoes he wore, even with his suits. The *Times* article had mentioned it as if it were some charming piece of eccentricity that could be expected from someone so young, so brilliant, so successful.

Well, Mallory would expect him to wear "real" shoes. She liked her men to look as if they could step right out of the pages of *GQ*. But even after mentioning Mallory's probable expectations, getting PC to look at shoes was a bigger struggle than Cindy anticipated.

At the first suggestion, he was starving and had to stop and buy them lunch at the food court. At the second store, he didn't like the look of anything they saw in the window and refused to venture farther. At the third—an hour and a half after they'd first started the shoe discussion—she didn't give him time to look. She just dragged him in.

"Price is no object," she said to the salesman and tightened her grip on Parker's hand. "He needs something basic and very comfortable," she emphasized.

"This is the flattest foot I've ever seen," the man commented as soon as he'd convinced Parker to take his shoes off. He measured Parker's foot. "No wonder you have a problem finding comfortable shoes."

Cindy snickered. She couldn't help it. The look Parker gave her quelled her laughter a bit. But as the salesman began to expound on the "advances in the technology of shoe design," Parker finally started looking interested. And she had to get up and walk away.

Parker joined her in front of the store a half hour later carrying three boxes.

"You found something comfortable, I take it?"

"No thanks to you," he said irritably. "You think my feet are funny?"

She giggled. "Hey, I wondered if you were afraid I'd find out you had feet of clay." She softened her tone secretively. "Hey, buddy, I already knew. But it was a shock to find out they were also flat."

"Funny."

"So you did find something comfortable?" she asked again.

"They'll do" was all he'd say. "Come on. Let's take these to the car."

They'd been making regular jaunts to deposit their purchases, except the suits. They'd be ready to pick up the following Tuesday after the pants were hemmed.

"What next," he said as they approached the car.

"You could probably use a few more casual things," she said. "And some dress shirts besides those plain white ones you insisted on," she added, surprised when he started shaking his head again. "You have something against stylish dress shirts?" Employees at PC, Inc. were allowed to wear almost anything most of the time, including jeans. Parker wore suits. Now *that* was something she'd wondered about, especially given his aversion to the shoes that would have been appropriate with them.

"I *hate* trying to match things," he said. "As long as I wear white and know which tie goes with which suit, I don't have to worry about it." He put the shoe boxes in the trunk beside the other packages and slammed it shut.

"Poor PC." She reached to smooth back the flop of hair the slight breeze had blown toward his eyes. "You do need a wife, don't you?" By the end of the sentence, the teasing tone held a hint of her sadness. That wasn't what she intended. Parker caught her as she started to turn away.

His hand lightly grazed her shoulder. "I'm beginning to wonder." His questing gaze searched her face as he traced her jawline and down the length of her neck.

The urge to close her eyes and lean into his touch almost got the better of her.

His lips quirked. "Is a wife going to put me through these grueling shopping trips often?"

She fought off her weakness and managed to nonchalantly twist away. "Having second thoughts, are we?"

"More than a few," he muttered, a touch of wry humor in his voice. There was a glint of...something she didn't understand in the warmth of his blue eyes.

"If you did it more often—" she had to break the visual connection between them to keep from stammering "—it wouldn't be quite so grueling. The sooner we get back at it, the sooner we get it over with."

"Maybe we can do it more often and not do any more today," he suggested, turning up his nose. Without waiting for an answer, he strolled to her car door and opened it as if she'd turned helpless in the past few hours. Propping his elbow over the top of the open door, he crossed one foot over the other ankle as if he was ready to stay as long as he needed to.

"I guess we're leaving?" She climbed in and

glanced up to offer a thank-you. He forestalled it when he leaned in, plopped a solid kiss on her upturned lips, then shut the car door between them.

She was still in a daze when he got in on the driver's side a moment later. He started to put the key into the ignition, then reached across instead to gently push aside the finger she'd raised to her surprised lips.

"Here. Let *me* wipe it off." His thumb started to firmly outline her mouth but his touch got softer and slower with each millimeter his finger traveled. "Sorry. I didn't mean to offend you with my appreciation."

Her gaze met his, questioning his brusque tone before he dropped his hand and concentrated on putting his key into the ignition.

"I wasn't offended." She realized how that might sound and quickly modified it. "I wasn't wiping it off." That was worse. "I mean...you took me by surprise." She dug deep inside her for the wry tone she'd used so often to disguise the depth of her feelings. "I was afraid you'd decided to practice on me after all."

In the process of putting the car in reverse, he rammed the gearshift back to neutral. His hand cupped the back of her head, stunning her again. "I'm not sure why you're convinced I *need* practice, but if I decide to practice on you," he muttered, closing the distance between them, "I assure you, it won't be a peck like that."

He angled his head. "It'll be more like this." His lips covered hers, parting them with a mastery that shocked her even more. He seemed to will her to respond and something in her clamored to. For a moment, astonishment and determination not to make a fool of herself won the battle, then she sort of melted. He finally lifted his head when all thought ceased and her hand curled weakly against his chest.

Even pride and common sense combined didn't stop a satisfied sigh from leaving her. Fortunately she didn't think he heard.

He was too busy looking smug and asking, "Not bad, huh?" He started the car.

"I'll prepare a testimonial for Flo," she managed to answer as he backed out of the parking space, "since *she's* the one who suggested you might need practice."

He shot her a look that said touché then sped out of the mall parking lot. Neither of them seemed to find another word to say for several minutes. She resorted to trying to convince him to order some "variety" shirts from one of Flo's catalogs just to have something to talk about.

She'd never been so relieved to see her little pickup when they arrived back at his castle.

"We have plenty of time," Parker had told her as she escaped the moment she could after the shopping expedition.

Parker had obviously decided they had all the time in the world, Cindy thought almost a week later when she hadn't seen or heard from him.

But that's okay! she told herself forcefully. The less time she spent with him, the easier it would be to adjust to the idea that he and Mallory would get married.

He *would* marry Mallory.

She had no doubt about that. Parker never decided to do something and then didn't accomplish it. That was one of the things that had made him such a nerd in high school. He was so single-minded. Focused. Half the time, even if he was looking at you, you suspected he was seeing right through you.

"You made him a list," she muttered to herself. "Why would he need anything else?" Once he had ideas, Parker had always been good at doing things himself.

And that's okay, too.

"Get over him," she lectured sternly, rousing herself to concentrate on the last calls she needed to make before she could put her newly remodeled house on the market.

Between calls, the cordless phone she held rang in her hand, startling her almost out of her skin.

"What're you doing? Backing out on me?" Parker's low voice said as soon as she answered it. It was warm, seductive, even though she knew he didn't intend it to be. His was a nice baritone voice that she could listen to forever.

"I figured you came to your senses about all this and decided you didn't need me after all," she said.

There was a long pause. "I'll always need you," he said, sending shivers down her spine. "Wanna have lunch?"

Thankful she didn't have to respond to the "need you" comment, Cindy glanced at her watch. It was almost noon. "A late one? I have several more calls to make before I can get out of here."

"Make your calls, then we'd better get back to work on me."

"I thought you'd changed your mind." She'd expected him to say something about him coming to his senses instead of what he'd said. For some reason, she couldn't let it go.

"Things have been…hectic," he said.

"I know you were out of town at least a day or two." Keeping track of Parker wasn't a problem if you only half paid attention. PC, Inc. consistently made national news in the technological and financial spots and those small items usually included mention of him.

"How'd you know?"

"I saw you giving the weekly luncheon speech at the National Press Club. So you had to be in New York at least one day."

"D.C.," he said, correcting her.

"You looked very fashionable in your new suit and the blue shirt. I take it Flo loaned you her catalogs?" He'd obviously taken her suggestion that he get a few of the classy looking collarless ones so he didn't need to wear ties with them.

"Yes. No one said a thing," he added with boyish disappointment.

She smiled. *Probably because the rest of the world dresses that way all the time and you looked normal.* "The next change will be more dramatic," she promised. "Believe me, people will notice."

"The haircut?"

"And the contacts," she added, trying to visualize him. It wasn't easy. "Did you get your appointment with the optometrist?"

"Yes. How are you coming on your house?" he asked, changing the subject.

"I'm finished. Well, almost," she said. "That's one of the calls I need to make. I have to let Monique know it's—"

"The Realtor you usually work with?" he interrupted to ask.

"Uh huh. I have to let her know it's ready to show," she continued. "At least it will be this afternoon, after I pick up the blinds I had to reorder."

"So shall I pick you up in an hour? Is that long enough?"

"Since I have several stops I have to make when we're finished, I may as well meet you somewhere."

"You pick *me* up," he suggested. "My office?"

"Sounds good," she agreed, excusing her sudden eagerness to get her calls made so she could see him again as habit.

"I have plenty to keep me busy until you get here. Do whatever you need."

What she needed, she admonished herself, was to get off this roller coaster of emotion she went through every time she thought of him. "In about an hour then? Give or take a quarter?"

The thought of seeing him pushed aside the thin veil of depression that had hung over her on and off since his announcement. When her calls went quickly, she stopped to do one of her errands on the way to meet Parker. If she wanted to wean herself from her impatience to see him, she had to be strict.

Rob Larson was her banker. After their three year business relationship, he was someone she considered a friend. He was in the bank lobby, shrugging on his lightweight coat and fixing the collar when she entered. He saw Cindy, brightened and threw her a wait-a-minute gesture, then returned his attention to one of the tellers.

He had everything Parker needed to appeal to Mallory, Cindy thought a few seconds later as she watched him finish his conversation and join her in the middle of the large rotundalike room. His calf-length double-breasted coat spoke of money, sophistication and success. His unhurried swagger and slow, wide grin oozed confidence and ease.

When Parker turned his attention on you, his brows scrunched together in an intense scowl. His head and shoulders bent forward slightly when he came toward you and he gave the impression of a freight train rushing you, ready to sweep you away. *Teach Parker to look more relaxed and easy,* she mentally added to their list.

"What can I do for you, Cindy?" he asked.

"I'm hoping to sign the papers for the new loan," she said. "I would have called but figured since I was coming this way anyway..." She let the statement finish itself.

His smile broadened. "You're just in time to let me buy you lunch." Somehow, he smoothly turned her around and steered her toward the door.

"I can't, Rob."

She didn't doubt his disappointment was genuine—he'd been asking her out on and off for two years now—but the expression he displayed was polished and probably the same one he used to fake the reaction. "You've already had lunch?"

"Actually no." She mimicked his regret. "But I'm on my way to meet someone." She glanced at her watch.

"Why is it that where you're concerned," he leaned closer, lowering his voice, "I'm always a day late and a dollar short?"

She laughed lightly. "I doubt you've ever been either in your whole life. Especially not the last." She spread her hands to indicate the building around them. "You do have a whole bank at your disposal."

"Filled with other people's money," he reminded her with his usual good humor.

"But you're the one in charge of handing it out," she pointed out. "Surely you can dole some your own way if you are a dollar short."

He crossed his arms over his chest. *Okay,* his expression said, *if you're so smart...* "So how do I fix the day late part?"

"You're asking me? The queen of bad timing? That should be my middle name."

He laughed.

"Which brings me back to the point: Am I going to get the loan?"

"I just can't do it, Cindy." This time his look and his voice was tinged with sincere remorse. "Bad timing again," he explained. "We both know you're good for it, but the bank examiner is due any day now. I can't justify extending another loan until we close the one you already have—especially since you're afraid this house isn't going to sell right away."

"Me and my big mouth," she said wryly.

"Your charming honesty is *why* I'm so sure you're good for it," he complimented. "Unfortunately I don't know how to fill out the paperwork so the bank examiners can see that particular trait. Don't you have anything else we can make look like collateral? The loan committee won't go for anything that looks risky on paper."

"I have my old pickup. It's probably worth five cents," she said glumly.

He shook his head, then smiled. "You'll sell this

house soon, Cindy. Quicker than you think. We'll be back in business in no time," he added. "Come on." He took her arm. "I'll walk you out."

He released her as soon as they were out the front door. "What time shall I pick you up this weekend?" he asked, starting their usual parting routine.

"I need a good banker more than I need a date," she echoed her part automatically. Rob was the classic heartbreaker. Good-looking, confident, probably the captain of his high school football team. Bill Baxter all over again. She knew he'd been a frat boy in college. He drove a snazzy car. A local magazine had picked him as one of the city's twelve most eligible bachelors last year. "I don't need the complication—"

She stopped short of finishing her standard refusal.

"—of wondering whether you're a boyfriend or my banker," he mimicked, finishing it for her.

Maybe she did. Maybe she needed exactly the kind of complication Rob would bring to her life. He just might be the distraction she needed to get over Parker. "What would you do if I said yes?" she asked, feeling the corners of her mouth slant in a coy smile. She'd never been good at flirting but she suddenly felt the overwhelming urge to try. She *did* like Rob. Always had.

He looked taken aback.

"Never mind." A hot flush crept up her face. She wanted to put her hands over her cheeks.

The surprised look on his face dissolved into a very attractive grin. "You're serious." It was half question, half comment.

She started to shrug it off but something stopped her.

"Saturday night," he suggested, not waiting for her to change her mind. "How about Saturday night? I haven't had a chance to consider what we'll do, but I'll come up with something wonderful," he promised when she hesitated.

"You really want to go out with me?" she asked, startled by his genuine enthusiasm. Over the years, she'd convinced herself his flirtatiousness was part of the service; part of his job. Giving his clients a nice ego boost made being turned down for a loan a little less painful.

"How can you ask that? You think I just crave rejection?" He said it as if he still couldn't believe his luck. "Let me think about what we'll do. I'll call you tomorrow and let you know."

"Okay." She practically squeaked it and her heart pitter-pattered a warning. *I won't sleep with you to get a loan,* she wanted to add.

"Don't worry, I'm not going to let this affect our business relationship," he said, reading her mind. "You still can't have the loan until we get the other one off the books." He glanced at his watch. "Now, you'd better get going or you'll keep your other date waiting." His voice left a question hanging.

"Old friend," she corrected, all the while telling herself she had to make the designation true.

He stepped down off the curb, bringing himself to her eye level. "I'll be in touch tomorrow." His mouth curved into a broad smile and she hoped the promised date included a kiss. One that would make her quit thinking about the one that still made her lips tingle.

CHAPTER FOUR

THE black glass windows of Parker's tall, dark office building gleamed in the afternoon sun, almost blinding Cindy as she slowed to search for a parking place in the huge surrounding lot. A heavy smack on the hood of her little pickup made her slam on the brakes. Squinting to see what had hit her, she was startled to see the door on the passenger side open.

"What took you?" A man with Parker's voice climbed in. Spots danced before her eyes from the glare.

"You just scared the life out of me." She still had her hand to her chest. "Were you waiting in the lobby?"

"Yeah. I called. Got your answering machine. Figured you were on your way so decided to save you the trouble of finding a parking place. That was forty-five minutes ago." He glanced at his watch. "And you were going to drive right past me."

"So you hit my hood?" She stretched to check and see if he'd dented anything.

"Got your attention, didn't it? Thought maybe you didn't recognize me. Don't worry, I didn't damage anything," he added. "Are we just going to sit here?"

"Where to?" She turned to look at him, blinking to get the sun spots out of her eyes.

"How 'bout across the street?"

Nothing registered as she stared at him in shock.

She was certain her teeth would have fallen out had they not been attached.

His hair had been shorn to a fascinatingly wavy half-inch length, all over his head. The glasses were gone. A broader grin than usual split his face. "So? What do you think?"

She blinked rapidly, making sure she wasn't seeing things. "You look..."

"You like?"

She was speechless. She'd *always* thought Parker was attractive. She'd never had an inkling how attractive he could be. The shorter hair and absence of his glasses let the world see the solid strength of his face, the determined square chin, the hint of his dimple. Prince Charming, live and in person. The usual Parker white shirt—but this one was nicely fitted instead of hanging loosely—made his shoulders broad and impressive. Maybe it was the stark contrast with his eyes as they sparkled, mesmerizing her. They were more glittering blue than the blue of a peaceful mountain lake on a warm spring day.

"You got the colored contacts," she noted more to herself than to him.

"These are the clear ones," he protested. "I followed your instructions implicitly. That's all you can say?"

"You...you look like that guy on TV," she muttered.

He was amused. "That guy on TV? There's only one guy on TV?"

"You know...that George. That guy on the medical show."

"George Clooney," he said, surprising her. Neither one of them watched much television. It was one of the things they'd had in common back when everyone else knew the weekly program schedule by heart.

"Yeah. That sounds right," she agreed.

"That's what the guy who styled my hair told me." He preened.

"The guy who 'styled' your hair," she teased, angling a look at him.

"You know. The guy with such a 'good eye.' You sent me to him." Parker had the decency to look sheepish since he knew full well that wasn't what she was referring to. "Styled" wasn't a word he would have used a week ago. "Okay. Cut it within an inch of leaving me bald. Who would have thought?" His head tilted in a cocky challenge.

"Yeah, who would have thought." She shook her head slowly. "Wow." She had to suck in a long, deep breath.

"I know," he agreed.

"You like the contacts then?" Her question sounded breathless.

He nodded again, then chuckled. "I'm still getting used to them. But you should see the reactions I'm getting."

"I'll bet." That very talented stylist had shown off his perfectly shaped head. How could getting rid of the bowl-over-the-head look change him from a geek into a Greek god.

Without warning, he was with her on her side of the truck. "We're rolling!" he hollered, tangling their legs to slam on the brakes when she didn't budge.

Cindy didn't feel movement until it had stopped. She sat, even more dazed, her arm around him, his face four inches away from hers. For a second, he looked as stunned as she felt. Then the grin that hadn't changed a bit, slowly tilted one side of his mouth and revealed the dimple she hadn't ever seen up this close. She wondered idly how he managed to shave the indent as his hand drifted to her shoulder.

"I wish I'd done this years ago." He leaned close to brush her lips with his...then drew away, lingering only a moment before scooting back to his side. His eyes sent warm sparks in her direction as if challenging her to say anything. He'd plead appreciation again.

Her heart pounded in her chest and she fought to get it under control. Why couldn't he wish he'd kissed her years ago, as she'd first thought, instead of wishing he'd gotten a haircut and contacts. Why couldn't the wish be for the kiss, not the advice.

A car honked behind them and Parker glanced over his shoulder. "Guess we should go?"

Cindy put the truck into gear, grateful to have something to do with her shaking hands. She couldn't help casting sidelong looks at him as she skirted the edges of the large lot and made her way to the exit.

The haircut and contacts had transformed him into one of the most handsome men she'd ever seen.

Mallory didn't stand a chance.

"Where to?" she asked again as she neared the exit.

"Across the street."

"The hospital?" She stopped at the street to let the flurry of cars pass. "You want to eat there?" He nodded as an opening in the traffic let her pull across into that full lot.

"They have a great cafeteria," he said, pointing to a car coming out of a spot close to the front entrance.

Cindy parked and followed him hesitantly. She almost didn't recognize him, for one thing. For another, she couldn't imagine that he knew where he was going.

He knew exactly where he was going.

"You eat here often?" Cindy asked as he stopped beside the woman on a tall stool by the register at the door.

The cashier answered her question by taking a card he extended and punching it for two meals at his indication that it was for the both of them. "The smothered steak's okay today, PC," she commented, returning his meal ticket.

"It's convenient and inexpensive." He steered Cindy toward the cafeteria line as he put his card back into his wallet.

"But is it good?"

"It's a hospital." He acted surprised that she would ask the question. "It has to be good, doesn't it?"

Stepping aside so she could go first, she waved him on. He put a tray on the line in front of her and turned his back to her. He'd left his suit jacket at his office. The white shirt seemed to stretch forever across his shoulders. Could getting a haircut make your shoulders look broader? she wondered. Maybe it was the effect of getting the hair off his neck, which made it look longer and stronger. She clamped her lips over an uncertain giggle.

The hospital cafeteria selection was more extensive than she would have imagined. There were three choices for the main course, every variety of vegetable she could think of and an array of bland desserts. Parker picked up a small slab of some kind of cake with a dry-looking blob of whipped cream perched on top as if it had been there for days.

Obviously Parker didn't know the difference between good and good for you, Cindy decided as they sat down at a long table across from each other. But maybe that wasn't so surprising, considering his mother had been the neighborhood's notoriously worst cook.

They had the large room pretty much to themselves. Two women in white—you couldn't guess nurses anymore—sat close to the door, sipping coffee and laughing intermittently.

A young man sat at the far end of the table next to them, his attention on the book beside his tray.

Looking back at her companion, she was startled all over again by his new disguise. She searched for something to say. "You wouldn't take Mallory somewhere like this, would you?" She swallowed a mouthful of the mushy green beans they'd given her.

His brows raised as he looked around, seeing the place through fresh eyes. "Doesn't have a lot of atmosphere, does it?"

Cindy laughed. "Not exactly." Somehow, the comment reassured her. Despite the way he looked, he was still the same Parker.

"You and Mallory have similar tastes." He twisted his mouth thoughtfully. "Do you feel slighted that I brought you here?"

She laughed. When they managed to get together for lunch occasionally, they ended up at some fast-food joint, usually close to the house she was working on. Her choice. She could meet him in her painted and stained work clothes that way. "It's a step up from our usual," she said, waving her hand over her tray. "Hey. A full meal? Complete with dessert?"

He grinned and stole a bite of his cake.

"What makes you think Mal and I have similar taste," she asked, still stuck on that comment.

"You always wore clothes alike," he offered as an example.

"I borrowed Mallory's things," she said dryly. Surely Parker didn't think she and Mallory went shopping together and bought the same things. "She has great taste."

"Oh." He blinked. "Oh," he said again.

"You look disappointed. What? You thought we had some twin fantasy going and bought clothes exactly alike?"

"No," he protested, still obviously baffled by this new discovery. "But the stuff you had alike—I mean the stuff you borrowed," he amended, "looked better on you than it did on her." His tone made it more a question than a comment.

"They did?"

For a second, he brought his hand in front of his chest to hover and circle. "Yeah, they fit you better."

"Oh." Even as she felt heat rise in her face, she gained some satisfaction from his gesture. Mallory had spent plenty of time indignant because Cindy, who was five years Mallory's junior, had inherited breasts from their father's family while flat-chested Mallory had received exactly nothing from their mother's side.

Parker smiled semiwickedly. "You were always more...more generously endowed." He sat back in his seat, obviously enjoying her discomfort. "You didn't think I'd noticed?"

Cindy opened and closed her mouth as if she were a dying fish, more surprised at his noticing than at the subject. "I didn't..." She spread her hands helplessly. "I don't...see what this has to do with anything."

"Well, your measurements have nothing to do with anything. But we were discussing taste. It would be reassuring to know I can't go wrong with this transformation. You liked the 'before.' Do you like the 'after' at least as much or more?"

She closed her eyes momentarily. How could he ask her questions like this? Was he determined to torture her? "I like you *any* way," she said simply. "But your new look is going to appeal to Mallory," she reassured him. "A lot! You look fantastic."

She could almost see him sit up straighter. Parker turning vain? She hid a smile behind a forkful of salad.

"So do you," he said.

She dropped the fork, splattering lettuce and salad dressing down the front of her best and only frilly blouse.

"So *did* you," he corrected with a laugh. "It's kind of nice seeing you in something besides your paint-splattered overalls."

"You like my French-dressing-on-a-white-blouse look better?" She blew an exasperated breath at her bangs and dabbed self-consciously at the spots.

"Guess I should take you to these classy places more often." He leaned forward to whisper intimately, "I always get ranch dressing with a white shirt."

She stared at him speechlessly for a moment. Then she laughed, too, which was exactly what he intended. "At least I stopped at the bank on my way instead of waiting until after," she said, giving up on the stains.

"Oh." He faked a pout. "The blouse and the nice slacks aren't for me?"

"As much as the haircut and contacts are for me," she said, lifting her chin slightly.

His unframed eyes shimmered with amusement. "Touché." He lifted his glass of milk toward her. "To the current version of us," he said.

She clicked her iced tea to his milk. "Now," she said, once they'd taken drinks and quit grinning foolishly at each other. "Shall we get down to business? Did you bring the list?"

"I thought you'd bring yours."

She frowned. "Do you remember what the nex—"

"Maybe we should just have lunch," he interrupted. "Whaddaya think?" Without giving her a chance to object, he continued. "Tell me what's been going on with you this past week?"

Something had happened to Parker since she last saw him, Cindy mused as she drove home later. Something besides the new look. What in the heck was wrong with him? Wrong was the wrong word. What was different?

He'd been thinking about the list, she decided. He'd been consciously trying to act on some of her suggestions, practicing. And today he'd been practicing on *her*, she realized indignantly. After she'd made it clear that practicing on her was off-limits!

That wasn't exactly what he'd done during their lunch, she calmed herself. He'd been polishing some of the skills on the list.

She'd told him he needed to be more aware of his surroundings. Less Self-Absorbed was what she'd written down, connecting it with an arrow to

Workaholic to show the two were related. The minute she'd written it, she'd been baffled by how they would go about changing it. He obviously hadn't been.

Since then, the one idea she'd had about being less self-absorbed had more to do with not hearing from him than anything else. She'd intended to tell him at lunch that he should make a point of calling and checking in with her at least every other day. She'd use the calls to encourage him to be aware of the world around him. She'd ask him about the weather; ask him if he knew who had won the recent college basketball championships; get him to talk about anything but computers or his business.

She hadn't had to. At lunch he'd virtually said nothing about anything except her. And now he had her scowling, too. She smoothed the wrinkles out of her forehead with her fingers. The man would make her crazy before she managed to get him out of her system and…married off to her sister. She pulled into her driveway.

Parker wasn't going to make her crazy; he already had, she decided as she realized where she'd stopped. She hadn't parked in the garage since they'd gotten the oil stains out. Now, after three hours of errands, she was sitting here like a zombie, still thinking of him. She backed out and off the end of the cement pad so she wouldn't have to clean it again. Nothing had changed yet; being with Parker still destroyed her usual good sense.

The phone was ringing as she let herself into the house.

"Hello," she said breathlessly, catching it right as the answering machine would have picked up.

"Cindy?"

Rob. It was Rob.

"We're on for Saturday night?"

"If you still want to." She offered him an out.

"Absolutely," he answered, a smile in his voice. "You think I'd back out now that I finally got you to agree?"

"I guess not."

"Good. I managed to get tickets—great seats—to the theater." His tone said he was very impressed with the accomplishment. "That road production of the show that was so popular on Broadway a couple of years ago? It's been sold out for two weeks."

She inwardly groaned and managed to be properly dazzled out loud. She'd thought he would suggest dinner and a movie or something. "Sounds great," she lied. She should have told him what she wanted to do. *Now* she remembered why she rarely dated.

"Shall we have dinner before or after?"

"You choose," she answered uncertainly.

"I'll make reservations for after then. Pick you up at seven?"

"Sounds good," she said again, wishing she could think of something original. "Let me give you my address."

"I have it," he reminded her, then lowered his voice. "We have to know where to find you if you default on your loan." But the way he'd said "I have it" made it sound as if he wouldn't have to look it up.

"Oh, yeah." She'd lost her mind. What was she doing? The man lived in a totally different world than she did. And never the twain should meet. In her efforts to get Parker off the brain, she was getting in way over her head. That was the *other* reason she'd never gone out with him. When she did date, she didn't go out with the kind of men Mallory liked. What had made her forget *that* little problem?

"Cindy," he said after what felt like a lifetime of silence, "Don't you dare back out on me now. I'll see you tomorrow evening," he added softly and hung up.

"Shoot," she whispered to the dead receiver in her hand. "What the heck was I thinking?"

Punching in Parker's number automatically, she managed to get her breathing back to normal before his machine answered. At least she hoped it was normal.

"Of course, you're not there," she accused when his voice kicked in with his answering machine message. "Why should I expect you to be? You'd think I'd learn," she muttered, already feeling guilty for her outburst. Parker had always been there for her when she needed him. "Call me back if you get the chance." The last sounded like a pathetic whine, she knew, even as she said it.

"What?" Parker's voice came on as she started to replace the phone on the hook. "What's wrong, Cindy?"

"Oh, I've done it, PC. I've really done it now. Shoot, I've never been to a play except a few of the old high school productions. You know, the one Mallory was in? And the musical my senior year because several of my friends were in it? I'm almost thirty years old and I've never been to a big Broadway theater thing with all the society types. You have to help me, Parker Chaney. What am—"

"Uh-oh, I know it's serious when you call me

Parker," he interrupted. "You want to start at the beginning and tell me why you're babbling over some high school play?"

"It isn't a high school play," she protested. She drew a long breath. "It's a *big* Broadway show and I goofed. I don't *do* these kinds of things. I run around in jeans and have coffee with the guys at the coffee shop."

"Okay," he drawled slowly. "But I still haven't figured out what you're asking," he said.

"You know those big Broadway shows they bring in from out of town and advertise on TV."

"Does someone expect you to fill in for the star or something?"

"No." She wanted to hit him for sounding amused. "I need advice."

"That I can give," he said. "But can it wait five minutes...can I call you back?"

"Never mind," she said irritably.

"I'll call you back," he reassured her. "I was getting out of the shower when I heard you on the answering machine. I'm standing here dripping. Can I call you back?" he repeated.

She closed her eyes to shut out the mental image of him standing there, wrapped in a towel. His nice, lean-into-them, solid shoulders looked satiny when they were bare. At least the interesting mind pictures had helped the panic subside. "You won't forget?"

"Do I usually forget something that's important to you?"

No, she had to admit. He only forgot to return calls when they were just chatting and were interrupted. In that case, his "I'll call you back later" was social shorthand and his "later" was when he had something specific to say. That was one of the reasons she rarely called him—unless she had something important.

Shoot, she shouldn't have called him now. This wasn't important. "Never mind, Parker," she said again and hung up on him.

When the phone didn't ring again in the next few minutes, she got irritated. Why, she wasn't certain. Parker took her—took everyone—at their word. He took things literally. She'd said never mind. "Why wouldn't he think I meant it," she muttered. But it was almost a half hour later before she left her perch beside the phone.

She went to the kitchen and started banging around pots and pans. There wasn't a thing in the fridge that sounded good. She wasn't hungry anyway. She slammed the freezer door shut with enough force to bounce it back at her.

She could call Mallory, she supposed. Mallory would give her the advice she needed. Mallory would also think she was stupid. And she was. Stupid and inexperienced.

Cindy leaned back against the fridge, letting herself slide down the front until she was curled into a ball on the floor, laughing derisively.

She'd spent the whole of her twenty-eight years, staying close to the old neighborhood, staying in some self-defined comfort zone. A wee bit smarter than average, she'd been promoted a grade when she was seven. Also a wee bit small for her age, she'd been younger and smaller than everyone around her. To top it off, she'd been daddy's girl from the very beginning. She'd liked fishing more than dolls, working outside in the small yard with him more than she'd like helping their mother in the house. None of it had made her a social pariah, but it certainly hadn't made her Ms. Popularity, either. She could have been voted Most Likely To Blend Into Walls if anyone had noticed her to begin with.

Mallory *had* been voted Most Popular her senior year. Since then, she'd been everywhere in the world anyone would be interested in going. With her second husband's resources, she'd learned to spend money confidently in some of the world's best shopping districts. Paris, Rodeo Drive in Beverly Hills, Fifth Avenue—stores Cindy wouldn't have had the nerve to step into.

Mallory regularly went to New York to see *real* Broadway shows. She'd been wined and dined and seen in all the right places. She'd even bid on a hat that had belonged to Jackie O at an auction. She'd sat in a restaurant at a table across the room from Brad Pitt, for goodness sake.

No wonder Parker wanted Mallory. She was right for him, Cindy realized with growing dismay. He'd grown and outgrown her. While she'd been standing still, lost in some fantasy that merged past with future, Mallory had been preparing herself to be exactly the kind of wife a man like Parker needed.

Mallory would know how to entertain in that castle of his. It wouldn't ring hollow and empty like a warehouse because she'd have it filled with all the right people and all the appropriate things. Mallory would know how to make it the kind of home a man in his position needed.

Mallory could go to New York and Washington, D.C., and not be intimidated at the thought of sitting beside him, at the head table at a press club luncheon like the one that had made Cindy tense, just watching it on TV. She'd look right, say the right things, impress anyone they met. He'd be proud to have her at his side.

Even with his nerdly, myopic ways, Parker had always been witty and wise and well-spoken. He'd made those household-name reporters laugh and applaud him at the luncheon. He'd faced their questions with his own down-home style, lacing his answers with his own brand of modest humor. No wonder she loved him. No wonder he *didn't* love her. He'd outgrown her long ago and she'd never even noticed.

Cindy didn't know how long she sat on the kitchen floor, her back against the refrigerator, her knees hugged to her chest, feeling sorry for herself. Just as she was lecturing herself to get a grip and get up, the doorbell rang.

Her doorbell. The one she'd installed and made work. "Let's see Mallory do *that*." she muttered as she went to peek out the peephole. She'd also installed that in the solid wood door.

She could have fallen through the gleaming foyer floor when she saw Parker standing on her small porch.

"You going to tell me what's wrong, or am I supposed to guess?" he asked as she swung the door open to let him in.

Cindy took one look at him and burst into tears.

CHAPTER FIVE

"ARE you going to tell me what's wrong now or am I supposed to guess?" he asked for the second time a good forty minutes later. They were seated across from each other in a corner of the little Italian place she frequented often.

"You didn't have to come over. Or take me out to dinner," she protested. "I was upset. I panicked. It was stupid. I was being stupid," she didn't spare herself.

Parker smiled far too much like he agreed. "You aren't usually," he said, "so you may as well tell me how you're being especially stupid this evening."

She couldn't tell him the truth, so she settled for half of it. "I accepted a date today with this guy at the bank."

Parker sat up straighter. "I guess I can understand why you are upset," he drawled at last. "Dating has always made *me* feel pretty panicky and stupid."

"It's not that," she denied. "It's him. It's where he's taking me."

"And where would that be?"

"To the theater. I've never been. I don't know what to wear. I don't know what to expect. Then we're going to dinner after. *After,*" she emphasized. "I could tell by the way he said it that it's going to be some fancy, smancy place where I probably won't even be able to read the menu."

"Then let him order for you," he offered dryly.

"Or if you don't want to do that, take whatever the waiter rattles off as the chef's special. They always have one. That inspired panic?"

"I'm a movie and hamburger-type girl. What am I going to do at the theater?"

"Enjoy the show." He grinned, showing perfectly straight white teeth, looking exactly like a handsome Prince Charming. He ruined it by scowling. "I suppose that sort of explains the babbling about high school plays."

"I don't even have any concept of what I should wear," she mumbled as the same kid who'd escorted them to the table and handed them menus came back to get their order.

"So now you want me to play fairy godmother to your Cinderella and get *you* ready for the ball." Parker resumed the conversation as soon as the waiter left.

"Yeah, I suppose." She laughed suddenly. "Scares you, doesn't it? How can I fix *you* up when I don't even know what to do with myself?"

"I asked you to help me figure out what appeals to…women," he said. "That's totally different from what you're asking. You're asking me to share experience. I can do that. I can help." He exuded that spark of cocky, confidence she'd been seeing lately. "Turnabout's fair play? Right?"

"At least tell me what would be appropriate to wear," she pleaded.

"You could get by with what you're wearing now." He indicated her good jeans and the lightweight fuzzy peach-colored sweater she'd donned after he'd insisted on her accompanying him somewhere to eat. "I'm starving," he'd said when she'd finished crying against his shoulder. "You can tell me all about this crisis while we eat."

So here they were. And he was giving her really bad advice. She could feel it. "I should go in this," she squeaked.

"I didn't say you should, I said you could. I've seen lots of people at the theater in jeans."

"The theater *and* out to eat at some…high-class place where I'll probably spill my wine in his lap or something," she finished under her breath.

"Don't order wine," he suggested.

"This would be appropriate there?"

"Where? We don't know where you're going, do we?" Before she could sputter another protest, he continued, "I've seen everything from jeans to the opposite end of the spectrum—you know, glitter and long dresses and stuff—at the theater. I suspect you'd be about right if you aim for something in the middle. Your Sunday-go-to-meetin'-clothes," he said, an echo of his mother. "That's always safe."

"That's why you wear suits to work," she realized out loud.

"That pretty much covers it." He smiled. "Where'd that come from?"

"I've always wondered about it. They *always* mention the casual dress code for your employees in those articles, like it's some big deal."

"It's becoming more the norm," he said.

"Since your company started it," she agreed.

"My company and others."

"But you wear suits—your Sunday-go-to-meetin'-clothes."

"My company dress code encourages people to

wear what they feel comfortable working in, within reason. I think it increases productivity."

"And you wear suits because you feel comfortable in them."

"Physically? No. Mentally? Yes. No matter what comes up or who comes to visit, I'm prepared," he said. "There've been a few surprises over the years—broke me of feeling comfortable in jeans early on in my career."

"But since everyone knows your company dress code, what difference does it make?" She shrugged.

"Mallory once said you could never be overdressed for an occasion. I've found it to be true."

Of course. He probably remembered every word Mallory had ever uttered in his vicinity. "Do you like your new suits?" she asked, changing the subject slightly. She definitely wasn't in the mood to be reminded how perfect Mallory would be for him.

"I'm very pleased."

She sighed. "Good."

"Now you want to tell me about your date Saturday night so I can help?"

She sighed wearily. "I like the man I'm going out with, but he's as intimidating as where he's taking me," she admitted, gnawing at the corner of her lip. "I should never have accepted."

"Oh?" That one raised brow again. That was something new. Or at least she'd never noticed before. It matched her modified, more sophisticated image of him.

"I've been doing business with him since my first house. He's the loan officer where I bank."

"The guy who turned down your loan?"

"One and the same." She grimaced. "I have no idea why I said I'd go."

"Because you want to?"

"Because...because..." She couldn't tell Parker she agreed to go out with Rob because she needed to get over *him*.

"Let me guess. He's good-looking, suave, very successful?"

"All of the above. He *is* Prince Charming!" she exclaimed. "When I saw him today, I thought, 'He's exactly who PC needs.' He could teach you all the things you need to know. Mallory would be fascinated with him."

Parker's expression had gone glum. "That good, huh?"

"He's perfect, PC. He's really who you need to...teach you things."

"Thanks anyway," he said dryly. "I'll take you."

"That's one reason I decided to go out with him this time," she said.

"This isn't the first time he's asked?"

"He's been asking me out since...since the first time we met, practically."

"Why now?"

The waiter set her pasta and his gigantic sandwich in front of them. "Can I get you anything else?"

After a thanks, Parker barely took note of the waiter or the sandwich. "So why now?" he asked again.

"I don't know." She was starting to feel like an insect under a magnifying glass. Once Parker put his analytical mind to something, nothing got past him. "You started me thinking, I guess."

He rearranged the bread on his sandwich. "This

has something to do with our conversation the day we went shopping, doesn't it?''

"I'm not sure what you mean." She was busily concentrating on rolling spaghetti onto her fork.

"You talked about how our friendship would change." He picked up half of the sandwich. He had a certain indefinable grace. His long elegant fingers held the piled-high ingredients in place, yet he managed to not squish the bread. It was an art. Few people could eat a sub without losing shredded lettuce and bits of tomatoes and cheese everywhere. Or they hung on tightly to keep the pieces together, smashed the whole thing flat as a pancake and then started losing parts—her technique. She never ate a submarine sandwich in public. "Maybe it's time. Maybe we're due for a change."

His words felt like a weight on her chest. But she knew he was right. "You've become very sophisticated while I wasn't paying attention," she said. "You are Prince Charming. With your new haircut, the contacts...and with Mallory...the world will notice now."

"You trying to quit on me before the job's done?" He replaced the sandwich he'd only taken a bite or two from on the foil wrapper. He laced his long fingers together and tented his hands over everything.

"I'm just pointing out that you're miles ahead of me, Mr. Chaney. You won't be out of your element with Mal." She used the childhood nickname Mallory had forbidden long ago. "Or anyone else," she added as an afterthought. "I can't say the same for me— especially with Rob." It was time to get this discussion away from things she felt far too sensitive about right now. Even after five minutes hiding in the bathroom with a bag of ice, she was certain Parker could still see her puffy, red eyes. "The very thought of going out with Rob freaked me out like some dingy broad. Crazy, isn't it?"

"It's the blond hair," Parker quipped. "I suspected its effects would catch up with you someday. You're the sanest blonde I've ever met. I've always regretted I couldn't use the jokes I hear at work on you." He took another bite of his sandwich.

"Thanks." She rolled her eyes. "I think."

"You're welcome. We are a pair, aren't we? You're terrified of new experiences. I'm intimidated by women."

"What? I don't count?"

"No," he answered far too slowly. "You're Cindy." His voice softened and he took the edge off what she should take as an insult with a wink and a smile. "Okay. Let's prepare you for this date with…with the *real* Prince Charming."

"Why don't you go out more?" he asked on their way back home. "You never dated much—even back in high school," he added. "But you had as many guys interested as Mallory."

His tone made her nervous. Once he turned his attention on a question, he didn't let it go until he'd found an answer. She wished she could see his eyes. "Now I know how desperately you need those glasses." Her laugh sounded uneasy. "Either that or you weren't paying attention at all."

"Most of the time," he contradicted her, "Mallory had Baxter hanging around. That kept a lot of others at bay."

Himself included, Cindy thought.

"Except for a few weeks here and there when they broke up, she dated him—or someone like him—every year, all through high school. Kinda makes you wonder how Mal goes through husbands so fast, doesn't it?" he surprised her by saying.

"Maybe she got in the habit of the year-at-a-time thing," Cindy said without thinking. She minimized any negative effects with, "Hey, she's doing better. This last one was five, almost six years. I suspect she just hasn't married the right man yet," she added softly.

"You, on the other hand," he stunned her again by saying, "went out with Michael and Sean and Casey and Donald—"

"Donovan," she corrected him. "And those little romances lasted all of two or three weeks. My record with anyone was three weeks. I could always figure out how to run them off quickly, couldn't I?"

"That's my point." He snapped his fingers and ended with his index finger almost under her nose. "You ran them off."

"It's a talent I have."

"Be flippant if you want," he countered, "but after one or two dates, you'd act...cold, standoffish. They'd see the handwriting on the wall and look elsewhere. If they stuck around for five or six dates, you'd flat tell them to get lost. And we haven't started naming the ones you refused to go out with even once."

'Cause I was always so stuck on you I couldn't see anyone else. "They were hanging around to catch Mallory's eye," she said. "I'm not a total fool."

"Maybe you could use that your freshman year, but after that..." He shook his head. "Nah. Mallory was well on her way to marrying that first guy by

then. I used to feel sorry for some of those guys."
She saw him wince as he drove under a streetlight.
She wasn't sure who he was flinching for, Mallory's
first husband or the guys he said she ran off? "That
doesn't explain why you don't date now?"

"I do."

"Who?" he demanded.

"One of the guys who worked for me last sum-
mer," she said. "We went out four times."

"Then you ran him off?"

"He went back to college," she said.

"Ah," he said knowingly.

"I was not robbing the cradle, if that's what you
think," she snapped. "He didn't realize he wanted to
go to college until he'd been out of high school several years. He was only a year younger than me. But
that is one of the other problems. I'm twenty-eight,
work mostly by myself and don't meet anyone who
isn't either younger or already married. Where am I
going to find guys to date? Of course there are the
ones you meet and know immediately, *why* they
aren't married."

"Like me, you mean."

"Yeah, let's talk about you," she said. "Why are
we hauling *me* over the coals? You don't exactly date
on a regular basis." The minute she said it, she
wished she could take it back. He'd been waiting for
Mallory, the same way she'd been waiting for him.
Did she really need to hear him say it again? She
tightened her grip on her purse, steeling herself for
his response.

"I get out occasionally." He eased his car into her
driveway and shut off the engine.

He *had* dated a few people from work. And there

was that friend of a friend he'd met a couple of years ago in New York. She knew he saw her sometimes when he was back East, especially if he needed an escort for some especially whoop-de-do occasion. But Cindy had never felt threatened by any of them. With good reason, she realized. He wasn't any more interested in them than he was in her.

"So why haven't you dated more?"

He grinned.

"Never mind." She waved away the question. "You think women are attracted because of your success."

He tilted his head. "I didn't exactly see them lining up before I'd made something of PC, Inc. Did you?"

"Are they lining up now?" she teased.

"Before." He posed, creating a rather attractive silhouette against the bright moonlit night. "Or after?"

"Before."

"I haven't had trouble getting a date when I wanted one. But I suspect it doesn't have a lot to do with my sparkling personality."

"Oh, I don't know, PC. The sparkling personality may be it exactly."

"Yeah, sure."

"You dropped everything and came to see why I was having a panic attack," she said sincerely. "That's pretty sparkling to me."

"Lucky for me, you're prejudiced." He reached across the dark car and took her hand. "You see my faults but don't hold them against me. That's how I knew you could fix 'em if anyone could."

She squirmed. His hand and his words were too warm. She wanted to fling herself across the space between them and into the stability and comfort of his arms. She longed for him to kiss her again. She withdrew her hand from his and asked lightly, "And after?" She had to push the words past a huge lump in her throat. "You hinted this afternoon that you're getting some interesting reactions to the 'new' you."

His laughter wrapped her in the warm, rich, melodious sound. "This afternoon at a stoplight, a woman in the car next to me actually whistled."

"You sound surprised."

"It isn't a common occurrence."

Without thinking, she reached across to smooth the back of her finger down his sculpted-looking face. "You do look more…accessible."

"You think?" His hand caught hers and turned it, pressing it to his cheek.

"You aren't scowling and squinting behind those glasses anymore. You look less…imposing." It was the only word she could think of. Shoot, it was a miracle she could think at all. Because instead of regaining control of her hand and her mind, she sat dazed, scared to breathe, savoring the intimacy of his late-in-the-day beard-scruffed cheek pressed against her palm.

He sort of nuzzled into it before releasing it. "We're a pair, aren't we?"

She wasn't sure what he meant but agreed with a silent nod.

"I'm so glad you're willing to help fix me."

"Now, who's going to fix me?" she wondered aloud.

"You don't need fixing," he assured her. "You need to feel more at ease with new experiences. And I *can* help with that. When did you say this date was?"

"Saturday," she mumbled.

"Then we have tomorrow," he said. "Be ready at seven. I'll take you out. Somewhere besides the hospital cafeteria," he promised with a grin she could hear even though she couldn't see. "Or a place like we went tonight. You'll see. You have nothing to worry about. And it can do double duty. You can give me my next Prince Charming lesson at the same time. Okay?"

"You don't want to wait for your next lesson until I've had the chance to study a classic big shot stud up close and personal?" she asked.

"Your banker buddy?"

She nodded then realized he couldn't see in the dark any better than she could. "Yes."

"Maybe we should have a before *and* after. One for you and one for me. How's that sound?"

"Sounds good to me." It sounded *too* good. All that time with him definitely wouldn't help her reach *her* goal. *Yes, it would*, she determined. What better way to get comfortable doing new things than doing them first with someone as comfortable as…as…one of Parker's old shoes.

It was time for her to grow—like Parker and Mallory had—and who better to teach her than him? *Then* she would go out more, find the courage to experience new things, and *that* would get her over him.

Parker waved a hand in front of her face. "Yoo-hoo. You there, Cindy?"

"Sorry. Guess I was drifting." She grabbed the door handle. "Thanks for dinner. And lunch. And…and everything."

"My pleasure. So I *will* see you tomorrow night at seven?" he asked as the overhead light came on. The

look on his face said he'd obviously repeated the
question more than once.

"Tomorrow at seven," she confirmed.

As for the clothes, she didn't take Parker's word as
gospel. She called Mallory, who encouraged her to
buy the basic "little black dress" and some "good"
accessories.

"Good, as in expensive? Diamonds and pearls?"
Cindy had asked.

"No, good as in coordinated and impressive, even
if it's cheap costume jewelry," Mallory had said.
"Think dramatic black button earrings with a matching necklace. Or some really stunning red beads and
flashy, chunky earrings. As long as they match perfectly, they only have to look good for one wearing.
Right? So it doesn't matter how little—or how
much—you pay."

"Right," Cindy said now as she fastened the pieces
she'd chosen to her ears and stood back to admire.

"Wow," she murmured, impressed with the image
in the full-length mirror. When Mallory knew what
she was talking about, she really *knew* what she was
talking about. Cindy had never seen herself look so
good.

The "little black dress" had been the toughest part
of Cindy's shopping expedition today. Mallory had
been very specific: a straight, fitted sheath, sleeveless
with a midthigh hem and no ornamentation. "You'll
wear it a million ways and never be disappointed in
how you look."

Cindy's one pair of basic black inch and a half high
heels made her legs look long and slender, almost as
shapely as Mallory's always did. If she'd taken

Mallory's complete advice, she'd have bought new ones, at least three inch spikes. But since she wore heels rarely and had only bought these for a wedding, Cindy had settled on wearing the pair she already owned. Not to mention, she didn't want to kill herself trying to walk in the ones she'd tried on.

The jewelry was the crowning touch. The earrings were an inch or so size graphic X, with one slash a shiny black and the other a heavy, expensive-looking silver. The beads were matching black with matching silver xs every seven or eight beads. She looked spectacular, almost like a model or a cover girl.

At least she wouldn't embarrass Parker. Or Rob, she modified, feeling guilty. She should be anxious to impress Rob, not Parker. Tonight was just…dress rehearsal. She smiled at herself again, pleased at her use of Broadway lingo. If she kept this up, she'd sound as much like a sophisticated woman of the world as she looked. She raised her nose slightly and practiced haughty.

It was almost a relief when the doorbell rang so she could stop admiring herself. The glimpse into this narcissistic aspect of her personality made her really nervous.

She'd seen Parker with glasses and the lanky hair for so long, she had to readjust to seeing him this way all over again.

"Wow," she whispered, then cleared her throat and mindlessly touched a soft sprig of the short hair. "Looking at you this way is going to take some getting used to."

"Wow, yourself." He grinned from ear to ear and stepped past her. She forgot to monitor his initial reaction to her, she realized with disappointment.

He blinked rapidly a couple of times.

"The new contacts bothering you?"

He laughed. "I thought they'd failed me totally. I'm still not sure I read the address right." He opened the door and leaned outside to check. "If that wasn't your voice, I'd think you sold the house to some stranger and forgot to tell me. Geminy Christmas, Cindy, what happened to *you?*"

She twirled self-consciously. "You like?"

"You are knock-'em-dead gorgeous," he said after a minute of just staring.

"Thanks." She damped down her pleasure. It didn't make one iota of sense to get carried away with his compliments. "Let me get my jacket." She'd found the lightweight black swing coat on sale, a perfect match for the dress.

He held it for her then settled his hands on her shoulders, easing it into place. She felt the heat of him, knew he leaned closer. Every nerve ending in her body tingled.

"You smell terrific, too," he said near her ear. "But then you always do. I love that fragrance," he added as she opened her mouth to tell him it was what she always wore.

She shrugged away from him, irritated at herself for enjoying his warm, familiar touch so much. Opening the screen door, she led him into a pleasant dusk that was rapidly settling into a cool night.

He opened her car door then walked around to his side. The man definitely took her breath away. On the off chance Mallory wasn't interested—fat chance, Cindy thought with renewed certainty—there wouldn't be any shortage of women lining up. Even if they *didn't* know he was on some magazine's annual list of the richest people in America.

Without thinking, she reached to finger his short hair again as he settled beside her. "Who would have thought," she said, blithely excusing—she hoped—her sudden proclivity for touching him, "your hair had that little bit of wave."

He didn't turn the key he'd just inserted into the ignition. Instead he laced his fingers through hers and eased their hands to the console between them. Turning toward her, his eyes searched her face.

He didn't understand what was going on. He was just realizing something had changed. She wanted to crawl under the seat. A couple of weeks ago, she could have smoothed his hair without either of them thinking about it. Now, he felt her unruly tension and it was contagious.

It's your imagination, something in her argued.

But he felt it, she was certain. It was there in the way he gingerly let go of her hand, carefully placing his on the gearshift.

He stared at her as if he had something he wanted to say, then confirmed her suspicions by opening his mouth slightly. His tongue sneaked to the corner of his mouth, then swept his lower lip. It was a gesture he used when he was carefully choosing his words. But the action had never made her mouth water before.

He'd never kissed her before, either, so watching him do it had never reminded her of the way his lips had felt against hers.

She eased out the breath she'd been holding when he nipped at that same lower lip, indicating he'd decided to say nothing.

With a baffled look, he started the car, giving the process more attention than it needed. Casting a tense smile in her general direction, he backed out of the driveway. "Guess we need to be going," he said unnecessarily. "Our reservations are for seven-thirty."

Cindy crossed her feet at the ankles and forced herself to lean back against her seat. She could at least *look* relaxed. She wished...

No. Wishing wouldn't make anything so.

"My real estate agent listed the house this afternoon," she said, indicating the sign in front of the house. Safe topic.

"I saw." She noticed his shoulders lower slightly.

She was making him a nervous wreck. Right now, he was probably wondering why he'd suggested this. Until now, she'd always been okay with waiting until Parker discovered how he felt about her. Somewhere, in the back of her mind, she'd never doubted that he would. Now that he'd shared his dreams and made her face reality, she was taking everything he said and did and interpreting it to mean that what he'd told her wasn't true. She wasn't being fair.

He'd been honest. He'd never once led her to believe he would want to spend his life with her.

Parker was doing this to help her. He wanted her to relax and enjoy her date with Rob tomorrow. He didn't have to take her out. She needed to appreciate his efforts instead of trying to see meanings that weren't there.

Maybe the first step in getting over him wasn't finding someone else to attach her attention to. Maybe the first step was accepting reality. She and Parker didn't belong together. It had been fact only in her imagination. It was time to accept that he would never love her the way she longed for him to. Reality. If she could accept it, then she could move on.

CHAPTER SIX

SMALL talk erased the tension between them by the time they reached the hotel Parker said was home to the most highly touted rooftop restaurant in all of Kansas City. He pulled in between an impressive fountain and the hotel's elegant entry as two men in long-coated red uniforms hurried to meet them. One opened her door with a flourish while the other stepped to Parker's side and took the car keys Parker handed him, then slid into the driver's seat.

"There's an added bonus to this place," Parker said as he came to where she hesitantly waited.

"Oh?" Cindy stood straighter and hoped she didn't look as out of place as she felt. The doorman smiled approvingly as he held the door for them and she felt better.

"I called around and several people named this as a very common place to come after the theater," he said, leading her to the elevator. "I hope you get lucky and your friend brings you here," he added.

Cindy didn't know why she was surprised when the maître d' greeted Parker by name...well, Mr. Chaney if you could call that his name, she amended the thought. It sounded foreign to her ears even without the man's fluid-as-expensive-leather accent. Parker entertained a lot for business. She doubted he took *them* to the hospital cafeteria.

"Why are you smiling that way?" Parker asked as

soon as the wine steward had obtained his quiet instructions and left their table.

"My, we *are* at home here," she taunted.

"My, we are quick at putting on airs for someone who professes such unworldly innocence." He quickly softened his own taunt. "That's what you're smiling about?"

"I get the feeling there's a side those of us who've known you forever rarely see."

He lifted one shoulder. "I've never really thought about it."

"You've *had* to learn things to get where you are."

He picked up the menu as a waiter brought their wine. "You know what I've learned?" He didn't wait for a response. "I've learned half the battle is acting like you don't have to learn a thing." He winked. "I'd say you're doing okay." He indicated the room around them. "For example, this restaurant."

Her gaze swept the room around them.

"It isn't really any different than the place we went last night. It's a restaurant. They bring you a menu and call things some fancy foreign name—usually something du jour—instead of the Tuesday or Friday Special. You order. Then you pay a lot for the food because they bring it on nicer plates and put it on a tablecloth and give you a cloth napkin instead of paper."

"And fine crystal," she said, boldly raising the wineglass to him. She took a sip, self-conscious at the way he smiled at her. She carefully sat the glass down, hoping the way her hand shook wasn't noticeable. Oh well. If it was, Parker would blame nerves. Never mind where they were. Never mind that who she was with was supposed to make her comfortable. She badly wanted to measure up.

"You look like you belong here," Parker said, reading her mind. "I'm not sure it's a compliment," he said almost before she finished her murmured thanks. He frowned. "Maybe that's one reason I don't mix my personal life much with business."

"What do you mean?"

He twisted his mouth, thinking for a moment. "I've been thinking about the workaholic thing," he finally said. "I know you're right. I know I am. But there hasn't been a lot to do besides."

"And you love what you do," she inserted.

"Yeah. I do get a kick out of making computers do what I want them to do." He twirled the stem of his wineglass as a familiar gleam came into his eyes. "Playing around with code is fascinating. Inventing my own is even more so."

"We used to go to movies or the bowling alley. Stuff like that occasionally." She hoped to keep him from getting sidetracked on the subject so dear to his heart.

He nodded. "What do you think happened?"

She had to hold her thought as the waiter came to take their order. "What did you say the Chef's Special was?" she asked the tuxedo-clad attendant when Parker arched an eyebrow in her direction to see if she needed more time. "That sounds very good," she said at his answer and handed back the leather-covered menu.

"I'll have the same," Parker said. After he'd ordered every accompaniment the waiter suggested, he grinned at her conspiratorially. "Fast learner."

"Good teacher." She leaned back and looked at

the patrons around them. The padded, high-back chairs weren't as comfortable as the booth they'd sat in last night. "Looking at it the way you do puts a new slant on things. Plus," she added, lifting a finger to make the point, "not looking at the prices on the menu helps."

He laughed. "That menu has no prices."

"That's worse." She shuddered. "I'm glad I didn't get around to opening it."

"I didn't have the luxury of worrying about this kind of thing when things started going well for me." He sobered.

"I'm pretty silly, aren't I?"

"Not really." He squirmed against his high-back chair, trying to get more comfortable as he stretched his long legs beneath the table. "But everything takes on a different meaning, depending on your perspective."

"I have no idea what you just said," she admitted with a grin.

"If you're lunching with the president of some company because you want him to package your software with all his computers. And if his company just happens to sell more computers than any other manufacturer, your focus isn't on whether or not you might spill your wine. Your focus is on how you're going to present your product and presenting it in the best light you can. You probably don't even have wine."

"You're speaking from experience?"

He nodded.

"The first time you came here?" She remembered the occasion, though he'd never mentioned the location that important day. He'd practiced on her the night before and then arrived at the house where she was doing an odd job that next afternoon. He'd been euphoric as he dragged her away to celebrate.

"I checked to make certain my credit card bill was current and that I had a big enough credit balance to cover a large tab before I met him," he admitted with a laugh. "But that's all I had time to worry about the first time I came here. A manufacturer I'd been bugging called out of the blue and agreed to fit me into his schedule while he was in town if I could meet him here."

"I guess I don't worry about what I'm going to wear when I go to the bank to talk to Rob about a loan, either," she agreed. "I mean, I try to dress appropriately, but..." She shrugged.

"Dazzling him isn't your focus," Parker finished for her.

"Yeah. Dating him is a whole other thing." Her sigh was heartfelt. Too bad she hadn't considered accepting reality before she accepted the date.

"You didn't take my Sunday-go-to-meeting advice, either."

"I'd wear this to church," she protested.

"Sure."

Cindy wanted to wiggle self-consciously as he studied her, leaving her body tingling from head to toe.

"But it isn't something I've seen you wear before. You usually go for..." He fumbled, looking for the right word.

"Something more modest." His gaze lingered momentarily at her neckline. The squared collarless style didn't show anything, just came low enough to hint that it *might* show cleavage. The subtle admiration in his eye stroked her ego. It was okay to let her ego be stroked, wasn't it? Giving up fantasyland didn't mean you had to give up feeling good.

She was delighted when the waiter brought the appetizer, saving her from having to blush or say something flippant. The man dished several stuffed mushrooms onto a small plate and set it in front of her, then did the same for Parker.

He shifted in his seat, brushing her knee with his as the server left. "I didn't know you had such nice legs," Parker commented. He *had* noticed while she'd been preoccupied, appreciating him, back at the house.

She was still groping for something else to say when Parker cut one of his huge mushrooms in half and forked it into his mouth. "Stay away from soup if you're nervous," he advised her. "Get an appetizer instead, one that doesn't have some sloppy dip or sauce."

"And ranch dressing with a white blouse." This dinner conversation she could handle without choking.

"See? You're getting the hang of this," he complimented, tongue-in-cheek.

"Except you forgot to tell me which dressing goes with black," she said dryly.

He laughed. "You do look good." Appreciation held steady in his voice. "Even if it isn't the kind of stuff you usually wear."

"Not that I didn't appreciate your advice," she said, "but I called Mallory." Cindy waited for his wide-eyed attention at the mention of her sister's name.

He concentrated on another mushroom, only glancing up. "Mallory's was better."

"She *is* coming to the reunion," she added.

That did bring his head up, but he didn't look any more fascinated than he had when they were discussing her loan at lunch yesterday. "You didn't think she would?"

She shrugged and helped herself to another couple of appetizers from the serving dish in the middle of the table. "I thought you'd want to know."

Noted, his expression seemed to say.

"She's about to sell *her* house, too," she said. "Part of the divorce settlement," she explained at the question in his eyes. "She doesn't want to hassle with lawn maintenance and the pool upkeep. All that."

"What's she going to do now?"

"She hasn't decided. She's debating between a condo and an apartment."

"I meant with her life." He frowned.

Probably look for husband number three. "I don't think *she* knows," Cindy said, guarding against sounding derisive.

He surprised her by shrugging. "Maybe she should settle for an apartment until she has something in mind."

"That's what I told her." *Or at least she should wait to make a commitment on another house until after she comes home. Right, Parker? She needs to be free to decide to marry you.*

The waiter brought their salads, taking away the clutter from the mushrooms when he went.

"Raspberry vinaigrette?" Parker commented. "That's as good a choice with black as you can get."

Cindy smiled. "Good teacher."

"Fast learner." They ate in silence for a few minutes while Parker scowled. His thinking mode, Cindy had named it and knew it was a waste of time trying to talk to him. Just when she decided it would be a good opportunity to remind him that he should pay *some* attention to his companion again, he caught her eye.

"Speaking of houses," he began.

"We haven't been speaking of houses for fifteen minutes." She giggled. "You might want to brush up on following conversations. Or maybe I should say continuing them," she amended.

"You adding something else to the list." His eyes narrowed.

"No." She waved the idea away. "It's there, PC. Just not in those words. Following conversations has everything to do with most of the stuff already on your Prince Charming list. Like not being a workaholic and paying attention to the people you're with. You have to go with the flow. Be *in* the flow. And mannerisms," she added, remembering Flo's addition. "When you're paying attention to the conversation and really concentrating on the subject at hand, your mannerisms are fine. You don't get the least bit self-conscious. You're very...graceful." It was the only word she could come up with.

"Thanks." He laced the word with sarcasm.

"It's when you're off on some cloud, thinking of some string of computerese or who you're going to market your next program to—that kind of thing. You're off on some cloud," she repeated. "Then you get jerked back to earth and try to touch base with what's happening around you. That's when you say or do things that seem off-kilter."

"Okay. I get your point," he said. "Now can we get back to my house?"

She shook her head and laughed again. "Oh, we're speaking of *your* house?"

He looked perplexed for a second, and she realized there were some things he would never be able to change. But it didn't matter. Mallory wouldn't hold his absentminded professor routine against him when he looked the way he did now, commanded all that attention, made all that money. And he'd gladly indulge her every whim.

"Come to work for me," Parker said, interrupting her thoughts.

"Oh, PC." She groaned. "You've segued again." She laid her fork down quietly. "What does working for you have to do with your house? Not to mention, you know I'd hate—"

"Not for my company," Parker said, stopping her. "I gave up on that one long ago. Come to work for me. Personally. Doing what you do best. I've been thinking about it. Well," he amended grimacing, "Flo and I've been talking about it. Wouldn't a legitimate job get you through until you can get another loan? I know I can't ask you another favor as a friend. I'd be taking enough advantage of you. But I know if I asked, you'd do it as a friend."

"I am a friend," Cindy protested.

"So let me pay you to do something you wouldn't turn me down on if I asked as a friend." He grimaced at his salad. "You know I do have to do something about my house. Furnish it. Fix it up somehow," he added. "I want you to do it."

"I'm a remodeler, PC, not a decorator."

"But you're between projects now. You can do my house while you're waiting for that one to sell."

"Pay a decorator, PC."

"You're irritated with me."

"No, I'm not. I'm just…I'm…shoot, I don't know what I am, PC. Why do you always have to keep me so unbalanced?" She loved his slow grin. She wanted to wipe it off his face.

"Are you feeling unbalanced?"

"Yes," she admitted and he looked disproportionately pleased. "I always feel unbalanced when I'm in this in-between stage," she said, hoping to discourage him from thinking he had anything to do with anything. "Finishing up one house, worrying about selling and looking for another." She waved a hand vaguely.

"I've thought a lot about this," he said as if she hadn't spoken a word. "You have exactly what I need right now and I have exactly what you need." He started ticking things off on his fingers. "You have time. You're between jobs."

"And you have?"

"Money," he said smugly. "Wouldn't you like to get ahead, then you wouldn't need to worry about selling one house before you could buy and start on another?"

"Of course."

"If you work for me for the next couple of months, furnishing my house…getting me and it ready for the reunion—" He interrupted himself. "Oh, I forgot to tell you. I called the committee. I *am* going to host the Friday night thing. So I *have* to get my house looking like something besides a warehouse." He used Flo's word and her wry tone. "If you do this for me," he started over again, "you'd go into your next project with a luxury you've never had."

"And that is?"

"Money," he said again. "Money for a down payment without waiting for the house you've just finished to sell. Money to cover most of the expenses for your repairs."

"You know how much you're talking about, PC?"

"I'm assuming fifty thousand would probably put you there," he said, proving he'd been thinking seriously about his suggestion.

She whistled. "Fifty thousand? That's a lot of money for a few months work."

"A decorator gets his or her fees from a percentage of what the job costs, right?"

"I think that's how it works," she agreed.

"I'm talking several hundred thousand to furnish and decorate my house, right?"

"Probably." To do the place justice anyway, she realized.

"So we're talking the figure I'm offering you anyway. At least ballpark. Right?"

"Probably," she admitted again. "But why are you so dead set against hiring someone who knows what they're doing. I'm not a decorator."

"Yes, you are," he argued. "I've seen what you started with on all your houses. I've seen where you finish. You choose the wallpaper and paint and stuff, don't you? You choose carpet for some of the rooms. That's decorating, isn't it?"

She nodded reluctantly.

"I'd rather pay my decorating fees to you," he said sincerely. "I liked what you did with your houses. I'm going to pay someone to do my house anyway, now that I've committed to the reunion thing." He took a deep breath. "I'd rather pay you. You know me. You know what I would hate. What I couldn't stand to live with. I know I'll be comfortable with the results when you finish."

She had to smile. He wasn't sure if what he *liked* counted. But he didn't want to live with something he would hate. He wanted comfort.

"And you get breathing room. It'll make your business profitable instead of a hobby you manage to make living expenses from. You won't have to sell a house for less than you need just so you can get a loan to start a new project."

She sighed. Boy, did he have her business pegged. And all this time, she'd thought he was oblivious; that he believed she was doing as well as she pretended. "I'd be glad to help you, PC, but as a friend. It'd be fun," she added. It would be. She loved the idea of having free rein with that house. "But I'd feel guilty—"

"You're turning me into Prince Charming. That's a freebie for friendship."

"Except for the garage floor," she pointed out.

"Except for the garage floor. Did you get the oil leak fixed?" he asked.

She shook her head. "I'm parking outside now so I won't mess up your work," she said.

"See, if you do something with a guaranteed pay-off for once, maybe you can afford to get your pickup fixed," he dangled another carrot. "Wouldn't that be nice?"

She didn't say anything for a moment.

"If you don't do it, I'll have to pay someone anyway, Cindy. I have to get it done unless I call the reunion committee back and cancel. I want you."

Life was so unfair. I want you. If he could only say "I want you" and mean something besides his house. She took a long gulp of lemoned ice water.

"I know you're not a decorator, but you're the right one for me." He grinned. "If it makes you feel better, you can do any wallpapering and painting yourself."

"New carpet?"

"If that's what you think it needs," he said.

She waved the idea away. She'd been kidding. A sense of excitement grew in her chest. She tempered it with another thought. "I'll bet Mallory would prefer to do the decorating herself," she said.

"Mallory is coming for the reunion. Won't that be a little late?"

"I guess." Cindy gave him a wary look. Mallory would probably *insist* on doing it again. Cindy couldn't let him hire her without knowing it. "She'll probably want to do it all again," she felt compelled to warn him. "Put her own touch on everything."

Something about Parker's smile stopped her in her tracks. "I already told you, I want *your* touch."

His low voice stroked her and sent shivers up and down her spine. "Do you want me to take Mallory's tastes into consideration?"

"Not necessarily."

Not necessarily. She let the smile start inside again then clamped down on it again. Reality was, he felt comfortable with her taste. Fantasy was thinking this had anything to do with anything but reality.

"Then you're going to do it," he asked as the

waiter cleared away their salads and brought the main course.

"I'll do it," she agreed. But this project, she was doing for herself, she decided determinedly—and for Parker.

When she was finished, she would leave a part of herself behind, she thought determinedly. She'd leave behind the part that loved him.

After dinner, they checked out a nightspot on the Plaza, intent on practice dancing, as Flo had suggested.

"I don't want to do this," Parker said abruptly as a second set of music started. They'd sat through one set and still hadn't made it to the dance floor. The band sounded as if they were playing their own cross between rock and jazz. "If I look like such a geek when I dance, why don't I do the obvious," he suggested.

"What's that?"

"Why don't I *not* dance."

"We could try somewhere else," Cindy offered. "Maybe we could find somewhere—"

"I have a better idea," he said, standing and holding out his hand.

She took it automatically.

"Let's leave." Placing a couple of bucks on the table for the waitress who'd brought them their drinks, he led her between tables and sighed in relief when they reached the cool night outside.

The stars were bright. The air was invigorating. His hand tightened as he laced his fingers through hers and strolled in the direction of the hotel where the car was still valet parked.

"Mallory loves to dance,"

"I know." They walked silently half a block.

The area was well lit. Lots of traffic going by. Lots of people milling. The Plaza would be that way until the early hours of the morning. It was the place in Kansas City to see and be seen, the haunt of the up-scale and upwardly mobile. Parker fit here. Mallory had loved hanging out here her last couple of years in high school, absorbing the atmosphere, pretending she was one of "them."

"Do you?" Parker stopped.

"Do I what?" She turned to face him.

"Do you like to dance?"

"Not as much as Mallory, but—"

"Isn't marriage about...about compromise and blending two people's likes and dislikes and... and..."

One of the area's horse-drawn carriages clopped by on the busier street behind them. The sound echoed around them, bouncing off the small canyon walls the brick and stucco buildings created. Cindy realized they'd turned the corner. They were out of the main-stream, still a block and a half from the hotel.

"Are you saying Mallory should give up dancing if you don't like it?" Cindy couldn't resist smoothing away the creases he'd pressed between his brows.

"I don't mind *slow* dancing." Without another word, he took her in his arms, hummed an off-key tune and swung her around. There was nothing awk-ward or hesitant about him as he danced her several steps. She felt as if they were floating on air, trapped in some mystical, magical moment, where she was graceful and beautiful. And he was the handsome prince.

In the distance, a woman laughed. Cindy glanced around, expecting the humor to have something to do with them and Parker's impromptu dance. There was no one in sight. And she suddenly didn't care if there was. It was heaven, being in Parker's arms. The sidewalk was a path to the bright stars.

Parker didn't even look. "I could get to like this," he murmured, urging her to dance with him a few more steps.

She was liking it too much. "PC..."

He drew her tighter against him as she would have pulled away.

In the light from the street lamp, she saw an unfamiliar gleam settle behind his eyes. "Cindy..." He mimicked her tone.

He mesmerized her. Her heartbeat got way out of hand. She touched the tip of her tongue against her lip, attempting to ease some of the sandpaper dryness from her mouth.

The movement caught his gaze and seemed to hypnotize and draw him closer. She felt his arm tighten around her waist. His other arm circled her shoulders. He hummed another couple of tuneless notes beneath his breath. To her ears, he sounded like a symphony.

They fit together perfectly, she thought inanely. His hard planes and angles molded and melded against all her soft places. She fit, right under his arm, next to his heart. It was utter bliss.

When his mouth descended slowly to hers, the kiss seemed like an extension of the perfect harmony, thrumming between them.

"Hmm-mmm," she heard him mumble, or mutter or groan. She wasn't sure which. It was a sigh, some active but robotic part of her mind decided. His lips parted hers with a sweet, seductive sigh. And he deepened the kiss.

Her fingers relished the feel of the stiff wavy sprigs of his short hair. She memorized the taste of him and clung to him for dear life. She probably would have stayed where she was forever—or at least until he pushed her away, as he would have eventually—if a car hadn't gone by.

The vehicle was loaded with teenagers who hooted and hollered and honked as Cindy pushed self-consciously away. She knew her face flamed. She kept it down, away from the blazing streetlight. *Get a grip.* With a huge amount of effort, she gathered her dignity, straightened her shoulders. "I thought we agreed it was a lousy idea for you to practice your…your…skills on me." She finally managed to lift her head.

"Who said anything about practice," Parker said.

Cindy swiveled and walked away, almost at a jog. She would have ran if it wasn't for the heels. She wasn't accustomed to the stupid heels. "Oh. And what would you call it?"

He caught up with her in several long steps. "Showing off."

"Oh." She would have flounced off again, but he captured her arm.

"You impressed?"

Darn, darn and double darn! What had she given away with that stupid kiss. "And what, exactly, am I supposed to be impressed with?" she asked with saccharine sweetness, then bit her lip.

"You told me I need to pay more attention, follow conversations, go with the flow. That seemed like the flow. Kissing you seemed like the next logical thing to do. I went with it. Are you impressed with how quickly I learn?"

She wanted to hit him.

"I must not have the 'go with the flow' thing down yet," he said when she didn't say anything. "Obviously I need more practice."

She *did* hit him, flinging the back of her hand against his arm before striding away. He caught her and twined his fingers with hers, tugging until he slowed her gradually to a stop.

She belligerently faced him.

"You wanna know something I've discovered?"

She shook her head emphatically. His amazed tone scared her. She couldn't bear thinking about what he may have discovered. He couldn't stay oblivious forever, could he? Not when she seemed determined to give so much away by kissing him like…like…

"You really don't want to know?" Wariness had taken over his voice. His eyes searched her face.

"No."

He sighed. "You ready to go home, then?"

"Past ready!"

Erasing his disappointed frown with a long, slow regretful smile, he wagged a thumb in the opposite direction she'd just come. "You're going the wrong direction then. The car's back that way."

CHAPTER SEVEN

HER DATE with Rob the next evening was a strange success. "Wow." He emitted a low whistle as she invited him in.

That seemed to be the phrase of the day lately, she thought.

"I knew you'd look great. You always look great. I didn't expect gorgeous."

She offered him an imitation curtsey out of nervousness. "Thank you, kind sir."

His admiration was exactly what her ego needed. Freshly slicked and polished, he looked pretty decent himself, but then he always did. Why, oh why couldn't he make her heart beat just a little bit faster. "Let me get my coat."

He helped her on with it, complimenting her on the expensive perfume Mallory had given her last year for Christmas.

The show he took her to was still playing to sellout crowds on Broadway, he explained. It was very entertaining and she enjoyed it a lot. The actors were better than in high school. The costumes more extravagant. The sets were fantastic. But knowing the players as she had in high school had made that experience more fun.

Her only tense moment came during the interval, when he introduced her to several of his acquaintances.

She could feel them studying her, trying to decide

if she measured up. Within moments, all but one woman apparently decided she did. Watching the way the petite woman looked at Rob, Cindy figured the woman wanted him for herself.

Afterward, as Parker had predicted he might, Rob took her to the same restaurant. The maître d' recognized her—how could he not? It was only a day later and she was wearing the same exact clothes—and treated her like royalty, though he looked at Rob speculatively. "Nice to see you again, mademoiselle," he greeted her before he escorted them to a table by the window.

Rob raised an eyebrow but didn't say anything. Tonight, they had a view toward downtown. Last night, she and Parker had been on the side of the room overlooking the Plaza.

Cindy enjoyed her evening. But Rob wasn't Parker.

"Well. What do you think?" One of Rob's arms draped the steering wheel. His other arm rested on the back of the car seat. His hand was inches from her shoulder as they sat in front of her house at one-thirty in the morning.

"I think I've had a wonderful time," Cindy answered, suppressing a yawn. "Thank you." She wasn't accustomed to two late nights in a row.

"Good. Then we can do it again?"

She lifted a shoulder. "Sure."

"Wednesday?"

She laughed. "Why Wednesday?" For some reason, she did not want to name a specific date.

He tilted his head. "I'm reluctant to let you go four days without seeing me. I suspect, with you, absence doesn't make the heart grow fonder. It probably makes you forget."

"I've given you reason to think my memory's that bad? Don't I always pay my mortgage on time?" She laughed again, fascinated with the flirtatious light banter he'd managed to weave through the evening. He didn't make her dizzy, looking at her the way he was. But he did make her feel good.

"But you certainly don't think of me between times when you come into the bank," he said. "So are we on for Wednesday? On second thought," he said as she groped for an answer, "how about lunch tomorrow?"

Suddenly she felt threatened. He leaned suffocatingly closer. She slapped around at the door, looking for the handle as she forced another light laugh. "Tomorrow? Sunday? I really can't tomorrow." She sighed with relief when he didn't press.

He was out his side, around the car and opening her door almost before she'd finished her sentence. He extended a hand, easing her out, bracing his hand under her elbow as she emerged. "I promise I won't forget you by tomorrow," she added for something to say. "I've had a wonderful time."

He released her by the front door. "I won't push too hard. You're obviously not ready."

She couldn't figure out how she was so readable. He'd exactly summed up her feelings. "Do you know how nervous tonight made me," she surprised herself by saying.

He gave her a startled look as he took her keys and unlocked the door.

"I had to call my sister and ask her what to wear," she admitted with a face. "I don't get out much," she added.

"We'll have to change that," he said, handing her

keys back. "I'll call you about Wednesday after you've had a chance to check your schedule."

"Thanks, Rob. I've had a...very nice evening," she said.

"The pleasure's all mine." In one smooth motion, he pulled her close. Her shoulders felt a pleasant but undemanding pressure as he wrapped her—not too tightly, but just tight enough—in his arms. His lips were warm and gentle as he sipped lightly at her mouth. He released her before she'd decided what to do with her hands. They splayed hesitantly against him as he set her away. With one quick touch to her face, he opened the door and held it until she was safely inside. "Sweet dreams," she heard him bid her as he pulled it closed behind her.

But she didn't move away from the front door until she heard his car pull out of her driveway.

Then she went to bed and tossed and turned all night.

She'd barely gotten to sleep when the phone rang the next morning. Bleary-eyed, she glanced at the clock and was surprised to see it was after ten o'clock. Unless she really hustled, she wasn't going to make it to church this morning, she thought as she reached for the receiver.

"Good news," Monique's bright voice said. "We have an offer on your house. A *good* offer," she continued when Cindy didn't say anything.

"I think I'm dreaming," Cindy finally said. "You want to hang up and call me back so I know for sure I'm awake?" She dropped the phone onto the hook then sat up and stared at it, waiting for it to ring again.

Her favorite real estate agent was laughing when

Cindy answered again. "I take it I woke you a minute ago," Monique said.

"That's why I had to make absolutely sure I was hearing right," Cindy said dryly. "I didn't want to find out I'd dreamed what you just said."

"You want me to call you back in a few minutes when you've had a chance to do your normal morning thing? Have a cup of coffee?"

"No. I want you to say what you just said again. *Did* I dream it?"

"No, dear, you didn't dream a thing. I have an offer on your house."

"A *good* offer?"

"Yeah, you heard that part right, too." Cindy could hear Monique's wide grin. "They've offered the asking price," she added.

"They know—"

"They know everything," Monique interrupted.

"Did we price it too low?"

"Right price. Right time. Right couple," the real estate agent said. "We got lucky. Real lucky! You haven't even heard the good part."

The good part? "They've agreed to the asking price. That wasn't it?"

"Well, that's one good part. But not the one I'm talking about now. The buyers have offered a bonus if they can have possession in ten days," Monique explained. The thirty-something couple was expecting; they longed to be well settled before their first baby was due, six weeks from now. And since the house was exactly what they wanted but less than they'd planned to pay, they offered an incentive to hurry things along. They wanted to move in before the husband started his new job in the area the first of the month and realized it might take longer than that for closing. "So they're willing to pay," Monique finished.

"And they don't mind about the halfway house?" Cindy asked.

"*That's* where we got lucky," Monique said. "Right couple. During the first few years of their marriage, they were houseparents at a group home similar to this one. They saw it as fate—like they were supposed to have this house. I think that's another reason they added the bonus. Everything was so perfect, they thought they might get *everything*— even the unrealistic thing—exactly the way they wanted. It was an impulsive offer. I *hope* you'll take it."

"Done," Cindy said without thinking. The couple sounded like the type she always hoped would find her houses. She put a lot of love in them. She dreamed a lot of love would fill them after she was gone.

She was smiling as she shuffled around the kitchen in her robe and slippers fifteen minutes later, making coffee. She delayed thinking about the complications the acceptance of the agreement might bring. It didn't matter. It would all work out, she thought optimistically.

The phone rang again as she poured her first cup. She half expected it to be Monique, calling again to say "April Fool" and checked the calendar before she answered. April was still two weeks away.

It was Mallory. They spent the first of the conversation comparing notes on selling their houses.

"Have you decided what you're going to do now?" Cindy asked finally.

"Actually I was thinking of coming home for a while," Mallory said.

Cindy's heart sped up. For a second she wasn't sure if she could breathe. She forced herself to take a slow, deep breath and managed to laugh. "If by 'coming home' you mean coming to stay with me, your timing is incredible, Mal."

"Not exactly a good time, huh?"

"I don't know where I'm going to be a week and a half from now." A week and a half! Reality set in with a bang.

"I do have thirty days before I have to give up possession of my house," Mallory reminded her.

"I know. I'm sorry. I didn't mean to sound like I don't want you to come." Cindy suppressed a shiver and felt guilty.

"By the time I *have* to move, you'll be settled again somewhere, won't you?"

But where? And in what kind of mess? Mallory had no idea the chaos Cindy's houses were in the majority of the time she lived in them. And furniture. She had one bedroom set, which she moved from one bedroom to another as she worked on the different rooms, a small living room suite, a TV and stereo, a dinette set—and her tools. She furnished at least one room in every house with ladders, paint equipment, an assortment of nails, hammers, etc. and her heavy-duty table saw.

"I'll *have* to be settled somewhere by then." She felt guilty for not urging Mallory to hurry home immediately. She sounded slightly…homesick? Cindy should be delighted Mallory was even considering coming home. When progress had demolished the old neighborhood, their aunt Janette, who'd come to live with them after their parents died, had moved back to Ohio to be close to her own children and grandchildren. When the two of them got together now, Cindy usually visited Mallory and whoever she was married to, wherever she was.

That was one thing Cindy hadn't thought about. When Mallory married Parker, their family would have a home base again. A *big* home base, she thought, seeing a mental image of his house. The idea was sobering. Shame that Parker might be the reason she was reluctant now for Mallory to come home made her say, "Mal, you come home whenever you want. I'm being silly. Where we stay isn't important, is it? If I'm lodging in a motel room somewhere, we'll share a room like we used to when we were little and whisper all night and it won't really matter where it is, will it?"

"No." Mallory's voice sounded small. She sounded touched. Touching her older, sophisticated and worldly sister wasn't easy.

"Has the divorce been rough?" Cindy asked gently.

"It has," Mallory admitted. "I know you didn't know Evan very well," she added, "but he was a really good guy. I miss him."

Then what happened? The words were on the tip of Cindy's tongue. Before she could say them, Mallory blithely asked about her date with Rob. "Did you dazzle him? Did you find the outfit we talked about?"

"I dazzled myself." Cindy laughed, then answered question after question about Rob and the previous evening's events.

"He sounds like a dream," Mallory said at last.

"What took you so long to decide to go out with him?"

Cindy couldn't tell Mallory why she went out with Rob any more than she could have told Parker. She couldn't even force herself to bring Parker's name into the conversation, she realized. "I don't know," she lied.

Mallory chuckled. "You hate *anything* new, my shy little sister."

"I'm not shy," Cindy protested.

"Maybe not in the classic sense," Mallory said. "And 'shy' may be the wrong word. What's a word for lacking courage?"

"I don't lack cour—"

Mallory interrupted again. "You don't have to stand in the corner with your thumb in your mouth to be timid. And don't say you're not timid." She stopped Cindy from protesting. "The last time you were out here, Evan fixed you up with that real hunky friend of his—we were going to have a barbecue so you didn't actually have to go anywhere with him— and you suddenly had to hurry back to Kansas to sign some papers or something."

This time, Cindy couldn't think of a thing to legitimately protest.

"Did he kiss you? Were there any sparks?" Mallory asked.

"He kissed me good-night," Cindy said.

"And?"

"It was nice."

"Nice?"

"I...it wasn't...it wasn't like..."

"Like what?" Mallory jumped on that slip of the tongue.

"It was nice. Fireworks didn't go off or anything," Cindy said, trying to push Mallory onto a safer subject. "I don't think you could say there were sparks."

"Did you give him an opportunity to create sparks?"

"I..." Cindy licked her lips. "I'm not sure what you mean."

"You didn't give him a chance." *I knew I was right* filled Mallory's tone. "What'd you do? Give him a little peck?"

Cindy sighed loudly.

"Okay. I'll back off, sis. But sometimes it's a matter of the right frame of mind."

Cindy didn't want to even *know* what Mallory meant by that. What? If the man had enough of the other attributes you wanted, you could close your eyes and pretend there were sparks? She and Mallory talked a little longer before they rang off. But Mallory had given her plenty of food for thought.

Cindy fixed some raisin toast, had several more cups of coffee and had just turned on the shower when the phone rang again. She'd barely clicked the Talk button on the cordless phone when the doorbell rang. Shoot, at this rate, she was never going to get out of the house today, let alone have time for a shower.

"Can you hang on a minute?" she said into the phone without waiting to find out who it was. "Someone's at the door."

She heard a masculine "Sure" on the other end of the line. She shrugged on the robe she'd just taken off and went to the door. Parker was leaning on the bell. She should have known. He didn't have a patient bone in his body.

Waving him in, she turned her attention to the phone. "Oh, hi," she said when she found it was Rob. Casting a glance at Parker, she wandered into the kitchen.

He followed. He pointed to the coffeepot and she nodded, acting as if that's what she'd intended when she came here in the first place. She left him to pour his own and headed back for the living room.

"I'm sorry, what did you say?" she said into the receiver.

"Sounds like you're having a hectic morning."

"I am." She sagged onto the edge of the couch. "Thank you for last night. I—"

Parker brought his coffee and stood in the arch dividing the empty dining room from this one.

She lowered her voice. "I had a very nice time."

"Only very nice? Never mind," he said. "I'll accept 'very nice.' It's a start."

"Would you accept 'wonderful'?"

"I'll accept wonderful," he confirmed with a chuckle as Parker rolled his eyes. "That's what I wanted to know."

Well, now you know. Thanks. Bye, she wanted to say. Of course she couldn't say it. She searched her brain for some bright, fascinating topic that was also innocuous. Parker leaned on the door frame, not even pretending he wasn't listening.

"I...I..." Brilliant conversation! Definitely fascinating.

"Have you had a chance to check your schedule for Wednesday?"

"Not really."

"Did I call at a bad time?"

"Sort of."

"You have visitors."

"Yes."

"Shall I call back later?"

Much later! "Yes, please."

"I'll talk to you later then." Rob rang off before she could even say goodbye.

"That the guy you went out with last night?" Parker asked as she clicked the Off button and put the handset down.

"Rob." She nodded.

"Must have gone well." His voice half asked, half answered.

"Rob's very nice. I don't know why I—"

Parker's expression encouraged her to finish whatever she'd been going to say.

"I don't know why I didn't go out with him sooner." She realized she'd opened the door for him to ask so hurried on. "You guessed right. He took me to the very same restaurant you did," she added. "The practice run made it almost easy."

"So everything was wonderful?" His grin mocked her.

"What was I supposed to say?" She sprang to her feet and paced across the room. "Men! It's like you all have to have some sort of score on everything you do."

Parker didn't look the least bit chastened. In fact, he looked pleased at the whole conversation. "How was the theater?"

"Pretty much like you said it would be. I'm glad I didn't wear jeans. I did really enjoy the show. Guess what?" she said, forestalling further discussion of her evening with Rob. "It sold." She spread her hands to take in the room around them. "The house sold."

"Already? You only listed it yesterday."

"And Monique showed it to a couple last night while I was out." She filled in the details.

"I thought you said—"

"Life is really strange sometimes, isn't it? The things you expect to be hard turn out to be easy. The things that should be easy turn out to be impossible. But maybe everyone has lucky streaks from time to time and I'm moving into one now," she said. She hadn't felt lucky the past few weeks. Parker's announcement had made it feel as if the world had caved in around her. Maybe she needed to take a note from his book. Decide something, then do it.

Instead of focusing on falling out of love with *him*, maybe she needed to focus on falling in love with Rob.

Parker was looking around him. "The buyers are the lucky ones...they're lucky to get it. They're lucky that you can take something that looked like this and see the possibilities. So what are you going to do now?"

"Go look for another run-down house to buy. I'm due to start looking for new possibilities." She snapped her fingers. "Oh. I should have told Rob I'd be ready for that loan sooner than I thought. He'll be pleased."

"Was he pleased?" He lifted a shoulder. "You know. With how things went last night?"

"I guess so. I didn't spill my wine or anything." She shared the joke on herself.

Parker didn't return her grin. "Did he—?" He jammed his hands into the pocket of his body-hugging jeans. Darn it. He did look good in them. It was easier ignoring his physical attributes when he didn't display them quite so well. Maybe she'd have to quit seeing Parker at all while she was trying to—falling, she changed the trying to—while she was falling in love with Rob. "You going out with him again?"

"He asked me. I suppose that means he hasn't written me off as a total waste. I *think* he likes me. I could like him a lot, too." Positive thinking. Exactly what she needed to do. "Except..." The "Except" sneaked out. *Except his kiss left me cold,* she finished in her head.

"Except what?"

Her face grew fiery, even as the idiotic thought popped into her head. But embarrassment didn't slow her headlong rush to stupidity.

"PC?" She stiffened her spine. It was exactly the kind of favor you could ask of a friend. It was the same type of request he'd made of her when he'd waltzed into her garage and asked her to polish him up for Mallory, wasn't it? "PC," she said again, "could you kiss me? I mean—" She cleared her throat and knew from the heat in her face that she was absolutely flaming. "I mean, could you really kiss me?"

She expected him to laugh. She finally had to peek at him. The mug in his hand hung in midair, halfway to his lips. "You don't have to." She swiftly released him from any friendly obligation he might feel.

He stepped toward her, a unfamiliar predatory look cloaking him, turning him into a stranger. An exciting stranger.

He'd bent his head in his single-minded, I-will-do-this mode. The wonderful blue eyes she could see so clearly now locked on her with an intensity that made her think she should run in the other direction.

"You don't have to," she said, retreating. "Really." Her mouth was as dry as the instant concrete mix that seemed to suck every bit of moisture out of her skin when she used it.

"Thought you didn't want us to practice on each other," he said in an amused drawl. Removing her coffee cup from her lifeless fingers, he set it, with his, on the low end table.

"It's an experiment," she managed to say and hoped it sounded flippant. "Not practice. I know it's silly, but..." She couldn't tear her gaze from his mouth. It slowly advanced on her. "You don't have—"

He startled her speechless as his fingers curled around her shoulders.

She licked her dry lips and the action drew his attention. The small space between them seemed to crackle with some strange electrical heat. He pulled her close, enfolding her into his arms, demolishing the distance, and the sizzle settled into her body, warming her and making her tingle from head to feet. *Playing with fire,* she thought abstractly. *We're playing with fire.*

His mouth grazed hers for a brief, heart-stopping second. Her hands tightened on his waist as he pulled away. She wanted to protest. She didn't have to.

"I'm not stopping," he said, as if hearing her thoughts. His eyes searched her face, then his head descended again. This time, his parted lips sipped at hers greedily, robbing her of breath, robbing her of thought. Robbing her of energy. She felt boneless as she clung to him like a lifeline, drawing strength from his rock-solid body. His hands splayed, roved, roamed, exploring the length of her back, the curve of her hips. He molded her to him while his wonderful mouth created magic.

Her breasts flattened against his chest, tingled, tightened. His hard arousal spread a scorching, fluid hunger through her belly. He lifted his head and she gasped, feeling deprived and bereft. She felt more than heard his commiserating groan. Relief rushed her when, instead of drawing away, his mouth grazed one eyelid, her cheekbone, a ticklish spot below one ear. He trailed kisses down the length of her neck, leaving behind mind-numbing sensations and spreading shock waves of need where they hadn't been.

When his lips returned to hers, one hand pried a gap between them and his hands took over the task of driving her crazy. He charted her waist and smoothed the satiny fabric of her robe against her midriff. His thumb brushed the underside of her breast. Her robe loosened and she felt the edges gape and give way to his fingers. They traced the fullness of her breast, grated across her sensitive nipple, molded and shaped themselves around the tender mound. His palm cupped her possessively, a perfect fit.

Arching her over his steadying arm, he dipped his head again, laying a path of tender kisses over the skin he had exposed, toward her breasts. She knew she had to stop everything, to pull away. Her hands clasped at the sculpted chest beneath his soft flannel shirt instead of pushing him away. A pathetic sound imitated a moan of pleasure, despite her opposite intent. "PC." Even saying his name mimicked a breathless plea for more.

"I want you," he whispered. She wasn't sure which affected her more, his words or the addictive sensation of saying them against her bare skin. Need shimmered through her and she wanted him right back—wanted him more than anything she'd ever wanted.

Maybe *that* would finally get her over him, get him out of her system. Would it be so wrong to experience his love—even a fake physical version—just once?

"PC," she moaned and his lips claimed hers again.

CHAPTER EIGHT

IF SHE let him make love to her now, how would she ever face either of them again when he married Mallory?

The thought slapped her in the face like a bucket of ice water. What in heaven's name was she doing? She pushed at Parker, pummeling his shoulder with the heel of her hand when he didn't immediately stop the assault on her senses. The second or two it took him to regain his control gave her the time she needed to gather her own sanity, to put his lapse into perspective.

"This is crazy, PC. What are we doing?" She straightened her robe, retied the tie, double-knotting it for good measure. "You're a man, I'm a woman." She lifted one shoulder. "I suppose it isn't surprising...things...things—"

"Might get out of hand," he suggested.

She couldn't look him in the eye. But she looked in his direction, past him, but close enough that, surely, he couldn't read anything into her evasive—

"We're only human," he added. It sounded very tongue-in-cheek and he was grinning from ear to ear. He'd backed away a step. No, she had. He stood in the same place, rocking on his heels, his thumbs hooked in the loops of his belt. There was a glimmer of unsatisfied hunger in his eyes, but it was tempered with something smug. She wanted to pummel him again.

133

"So what do you think?"

"What do I think?"

"The experiment, how'd it go? Did you discover anything?" he asked.

She'd learned she was still madly in love with him, she thought with an inward groan. Darn it. And darn him. Why wouldn't her heart accept that there was no hope? If it did, it would break, she answered herself. *She* would break. How would she ever stand by and watch him with Mallory.

"The experiment was very informative, thank you." She lifted her chin, expelling the traitorous thoughts running through it. She brushed her hands together as if she could dust the tingle of touching him off her fingertips. When he married Mallory, Cindy would leave town! Move. Go somewhere else. The experiment had been successful, she thought helplessly. Kissing Parker proved she could never, ever care for Rob the same way. His kiss had left her cold. All the positive thinking and decisiveness in the world wasn't going to change that.

"Did I measure up?"

"Measure up?"

"You're starting to repeat everything, Cindy. Is that a new habit?" He reached to stroke her face in the same affectionate way he'd touched her a thousand times. She backed away and he let his hand hang for a second before dropping it to his side. "How did he compare? Isn't that what the experiment was all about? A comparison?"

"You were right the first time," she said, grasping at straws. "It wasn't an experiment. It was practice. I...I wasn't thinking.... After last night I figured I needed more experience. Experiment. See? Similar words? But 'practice' was the right term. Thanks for helping me brush up."

She started to slip past him. "I'm going to take a shower. You can get yourself another cup of coffee or you can go—"

His fingers curled around her upper arm, delaying her retreat. "He didn't like the way you kiss?"

"I didn't ask. But he sure knew what he was doing," she threw in for good measure. "I didn't think it would hurt me to…to brush up," she repeated.

"Then maybe I should offer pointers. Do you want to know—"

She blinked hard and stared at him. "Not really," she managed to say blithely. "The way you got carried away, I must be doing okay."

"*I* got carried—" Clamping his mouth shut, he cut the protest short. She could almost hear him give himself his keep-your-mouth-shut lecture. He'd always said it was more important to know when to say something than knowing what to say.

Cindy eased her arm from his light grasp. "I think I'll go take my shower." She marched off, head high. One step from the hall and calming concealment, his voice stopped her again.

"What are we going to do with the rest of the day?"

She shrugged and started to say she hadn't thought about it. Then she remembered. "I will probably call Monique and ask her to take me to look at houses. She probably has a few things in mind for my next venture."

"That doesn't seem logical." He frowned as soon as he said it. She could see him mentally noting his slip.

"It's okay, PC." She couldn't help a quiet grin. "You can *think* logically and even say the word from time to time. Flo and I just suggested you don't say it to justify *everything.*" She leaned against the wall, the weakness in her knees from their recent encounter catching up with her again. "Looking for a house sounds pretty logical to me," she added. "You did understand about the bonus? I have to be out of here in ten days."

"Why change what has worked so well so far?" he asked.

It was her turn to scowl.

"You *always* live in the house you're working on. My house is still your next project, isn't it?"

She hadn't even thought of his house. "Yes, but—"

"Move in with me. Take over the staff apartment downstairs, if you want."

Cindy's pulse roared in her ears. Her dreams come true. *Now* he asked...but not because he wanted to share her life. Not because he wanted a repeat performance of a few minutes ago and wanted to kiss her senseless every day and every night of his life. He wanted help remodeling his home, winning her sister. "Oh, sure. That would—"

"You yourself said five families could live there without ever seeing each other."

Was he pointing out he didn't want to see her? Promising he wasn't interested in a repeat performance if that was what she was worried about?

"You may as well take advantage of the situation," he finished.

He'd probably remembered that Mallory stayed with her the rare instances she came back to town.

Having Cindy under his roof when it came time for the reunion would almost guarantee he'd have Mallory under his wing full-time, too.

"I'll be done furnishing and decorating your house long before the reunion," she warned him.

"What does that have to do with anything?"

"I...it..." She couldn't accuse him of the ulterior motives she'd just assigned to him because he obviously didn't see the connection. "Nothing."

"I thought you might not want to rush into something," he said. "Buying a house and moving in ten days is a pretty big rush. Wouldn't you prefer to have time to investigate the neighborhood, do a little long-range planning. Don't you usually do some kind of cost analysis before you choose a house to remodel?"

"Of course." She stiffened her spine. "I always do that." She waved at the house around her. "But it didn't guarantee anything with this house, did it?"

"Just trying to help." He raked his fingers through his hair, stopped short for a second by the unfamiliar feel of his cropped strands. "I hate to see you abandon a solid business practice just because you don't have time. Plus, I thought you'd save time and energy on my house, working on site. Save you some hassle."

He was half right. Living in his house while she was working on it would save driving time each day and make it convenient to take measurements, compare color samples, be on hand for deliveries, etc. But knowing he was close at hand would take double any energy she saved.

But ten days to move instead of ten days to do everything: find a house, check it out, decide what you have to do to it to make it a worthwhile investment *and* move. It was a luxury she hadn't counted on. "I could be working on your house while I'm looking around for my next project."

"Doesn't that sound logi…reasonable? It isn't like I don't have room." His familiar dry tone eased some of the tension between them.

"You're right, PC. It sounds very logical. I appreciate the offer. Let me think it through while I take my shower."

"I'll get another cup of coffee and read your Sunday paper," he announced.

"You do that." She started down the hall again, her ego and emotions bruised and battered but still walking on her own two feet. The way things were going, that had to be progress.

For the next couple of weeks, Cindy never *stopped* feeling bruised and battered. Fortunately, most of it was physical, from moving her tools and meager household possessions to Parker's. Transforming his empty shell into a castle seemed like child's play after the physical labor she was accustomed to.

"What are you doing?" Parker's voice startled her as she backed down the ladder she'd been standing on while she installed a new curtain rod.

"You're lucky I wasn't on top. You'd be picking me up off the floor." Cindy stumbled more than descended the last few steps. Parker's hands braced her and became part of the problem. The unexpected touch made her knees weak. "What do you think?"

"Of the curtain rod?" He lifted one shoulder. "It's attractive as curtain rods go, I suppose."

She playfully slapped his arm. "Of the way this place is looking." She looked around the huge sunken living room that was the center of the house. Everything else radiated out from it. ''Wait till you see the drapes they're delivering to put on the curtain rod in the morning.'' She moved away from the hand he'd lightly pressed to her waist. She was on flat, solid ground now. She could surely stand on her own. ''You aren't going to believe how good this room will look.'' She'd had to have them specially made to fit the massive wall of windows.

''I don't believe it now.'' He flopped onto one of his new couches and indicated the space beside him. ''Sit.''

Out of habit, she checked her jeans for sawdust, paint smears and dust. Doing this kind of job for Parker had its special advantages. Being clean most of the time was one of them.

She eased herself to the opposite end of the over-sized piece of furniture. It had to be oversized to fit the room. The blue-and-gray fabric covering it was perfect. The large plaid hinted at the casual style Parker lived. The silvery thread running through the pattern gave the sofa just the touch of formality it needed to be appropriate here. The tone on tone grays matched the carpet. And the blue matched his eyes.

His eyes. They smiled at her.

''You like what I'm doing,'' she confirmed as much as asked.

''I knew you'd do it right. I should have hired you the minute I moved in.'' He draped his arm over the back of the couch. Its size kept his hand from brushing her arm but she felt the possibility of his touch anyway. ''I also like having you here when I come home.''

He had to quit saying things like that. He'd been

saying lots of them and every one of them made her a nervous wreck.

"I didn't realize how isolated I'd become."

She searched for an appropriately flippant response and none came to mind so she changed the subject. "Oh. I didn't tell you. I talked to Mallory yesterday." On second thought, she guessed she hadn't really changed the subject. Wasn't Mallory the answer to his isolation?

His "Oh?" was almost disinterested.

"She got quite a bit of mileage out of knowing we'd 'moved in together.' Her words, not mine," Cindy quickly defended. "I told her I was staying with you until I found another house to work on."

"And she believed you?"

"It took me a while to convince her there wasn't anything 'romantic—'" she made a face for his benefit "—going on between us."

"Oh." He looked...disappointed?

Was he hoping Mallory would be jealous? The look he was giving her made her want to squirm. "Rob wasn't much easier," she added in self-defense. "He believed it after he picked me up last Friday evening. I had him pick me up here instead of meeting him somewhere. He came to the little carport entrance and I showed him around my little suite." Except the bedroom. He probably would have taken it as some kind of invitation. The whole date had shown her that Friday was her fourth and final date with Rob. He was beginning to expect a whole lot more than she would ever be interested in giving. "He saw for himself that you and I didn't even have to see each other to live in the same house. He realized the setup is more like I'm a favored employee than like we're 'living together.'"

A muscle in Parker's jaw twitched. "You told him you're a favored employee?"

"Just to explain the living arrangement," she said. "I said that's what it's like here."

For some reason, Parker didn't like that comment. "That must have eased his mind." His derisive tone grated on her nerves.

It reassured him I'm fair game. It made his hands roam a lot more confidently. "Since he didn't have anything to worry about in the first place, he didn't need his mind eased. Rob knows we're good friends. Have been most of our lives." She lifted one shoulder. "I told him you were like family. You'd probably be my brother-in-law someday."

Parker got up and stuffed his hands into the pocket of his slacks, flaring his jacket out behind him. Though it ruined the graceful line of his body—he looked so good in his new, perfectly fitting suits—it made him seem very male, aggressive. Dangerous.

Gazing at him made her mouth water.

"I'm sure he found *that* comforting."

"Why would he need comfort over anything to do with you and me?" Cindy didn't understand why Parker was worrying about what Rob might think. Shouldn't he be worrying about Ma—

"Oh, of course not. Why would Prince Charming himself need anything. I hope you've learned all his special tricks by now so you can teach me," he said, a strange note in his voice.

"Not a thing," she denied, aware that somehow, they'd drifted onto unsteady ground. "I haven't learned a thing," she said again. "Except—"

He closed the few feet between them and stood in front of her still as challenging as before. "Except?"

"Except that you don't need me."

Parker's scornful chuckle baffled her. She usually loved the sound of his laughter, but this time she didn't understand it.

"So you think I'm perfect now?"

"Nobody's perfect." But he was as close as you could get, she thought. "But sometime when I wasn't looking, you smoothed the rough edges and became exactly who and what you want to be." She had the courage to face him. "Rob has nothing on you."

His mouth curved strangely.

"The haircut." She absently pointed toward her head. "The contacts, that's just window dressing. You're no longer tall and gangly. Well, you're still tall," she amended as his lips quirked. *And devastatingly handsome.* "But you aren't awkward or self-conscious about it like you were when you were younger." Her mouth went dry. "It's been a long, long time since you stalked across a room with your shoulders slumped, studying the floor like you were searching for some elusive puzzle piece. You don't say egghead things out of the blue that no one understands."

"What about all that stuff on the list?" he asked.

She'd written a list, mentioned a few things. Parker had tackled each and every item, changing little things so subtly that she'd hardly noticed. But he hadn't needed to change in the first place. He'd just needed a little polish. And some incentive—like knowing Mallory would be coming back home soon.

He'd changed from the high school nerd long ago—all by himself—and she hadn't realized it.

Hadn't *wanted* to realize it, she thought with a sharp blast of clarity. She hadn't wanted to accept that he'd outgrown her.

She stood, intending to push past him, put some distance between them.

He blocked her exit. Close. Too close. He was standing in a very un-Parker-like way. Very unpolitically correct. Hadn't he heard about invading someone's personal space? Very un-Parker Chaney. The Parker Chaney she knew didn't press, didn't make his friends uncomfortable. Very un-Prince Charmingly. *Very* Prince Charming, she realized. Very...seductive. The way he looked from her eyes to her lips made her long to be swept up in his arms and carried away to some...some place she'd conjured in her dreams.

"You've been a very appealing man for a long, long time," she murmured, then cleared her throat, scared she'd given too much away again. "Mallory would have fallen in love with you five years ago had you been around." Mallory was a good name to throw in when she was out of her depth with him.

"You don't think I have anything else to learn?"

"No, PC." It was becoming impossible to concentrate with her pulse pounding in her ears the way it was. It was really getting bad when she could feel his electrifying touch without him even touching her. She swiveled sideways, moving away quickly.

He followed, stopping only when she reached the vast expanse of windows and couldn't go farther. "You came up with all that stuff despite the fact you think I'm wonderful just as I am."

She stared without really seeing the dusk as it settled over the parklike setting outdoors. Freshly budded trees and sloping woodland, with city lights winking to life in the distance held her gaze but not her attention. Without looking, she could feel the half step he took, moving more to her side.

"I made it up. From memory, from who you *used* to be, not who you are now." Anything nerdish about Parker had more to do with leftover images than reality. Nerds existed only in youth when people worried about such nonsensical things as conforming…and maybe lingered in the minds of those, like Parker, formerly classified that way. "Any tiny remnants of that person Mallory ignored in high school, you've annihilated. After Flo and I pointed them out, of course." If she abandoned the bantering tone they'd used on each other for years, she'd really give herself away. She turned and out of habit, started to smooth a strand of hair that no longer needed smoothing. Her hand froze an inch from her target. What was she doing?

His eyes seemed to ask her the same thing.

"Any shortcomings you have—things other people would consider shortcomings—are so minor. Experience has taught you so much." She waved her hand vaguely before she dropped it to her side.

Parker swung around and frowned at the view she'd been staring at moments before. She watched a muscle twitch in the side of his jaw. "Experience *should* have taught me a few things, but I did come up with this ridiculous idea."

"I warned you I wouldn't be much help remodeling you." How could you successfully transform someone you thought was almost perfect in the first place.

"That's not what I meant." He cast her a derisive smile then jammed his hands into the pockets of his slacks and went back to staring out the window. "You and Flo did try to warn me that I was approaching this reunion thing in some juvenile fog. Fantasizing about marrying someone I haven't seen in nearly ten years isn't practical, let alone feasible."

"Oh." She'd thought he'd realized asking for her help had been useless. It was the whole idea. He was losing his nerve. "Don't you do this to me now, PC," she threatened. "You've always been my role model when it comes to going after your dreams. You always make them come true. How do you think I've had the nerve to do what I want to do? If you give up now, you're going to blow that whole image for me." This time she didn't hesitate to lay her hand over his arm. He needed encouragement. That was a whole lot different than her just selfishly wanting to touch him.

"Dreams are worthless if it's what you do in your sleep. Or out of habit," he added with a grimace. "That's exactly what this was. An outlandish, impractical dream." He swiveled on her. "I've been trying to tell you since that night at the Plaza, I've changed my mind. I've come to my senses," he added. "I've realized I don't want Mal—"

"You two ready for dinner?" Flo's voice interrupted from the side of the room edging the kitchen.

Cindy guiltily jerked her hand back to her side.

"I asked Flo to make us a fancy dinner so we could try out the fancy new dining-room furniture," he said, slanting his head apologetically. "You'll join me?"

She couldn't join him. She wasn't getting over him. Her infatuation was getting worse. Cindy was madly fantasizing that he'd been about to say he'd realized he didn't want Mallory at all; he wanted her. From their conversation so far, anyone would know he'd been about to say he didn't want Mallory if she couldn't accept him as he was.

"I have a date." She glanced at her watch and gasped. "Oh, darn, I'm going to be late. Flo, I'm sorry," she offered her regrets and charged in the direction of the basement stairs and the sanctuary of her "staff" apartment. "I wish one of you would have warned me," she added over her shoulder. "I wouldn't have missed a test run of the new dining-room furniture for anything." Shoot, it sounded good. But a lie was a lie was a lie and she could feel herself flushing as she sent a contrite grimace their way.

Flo stood there looking pleased for some inexplicable reason and Cindy nearly tripped over her own feet in her impatience to escape.

"Oh!" She snapped her fingers and turned back to Parker. "I'm sorry. I...could you...would you mind taking my ladder back to the storage room downstairs. I'm sorry. I was going to put it up," she apologized again.

"No problem." He said it almost too quietly to be heard. The scowl on his face was...mystifying.

And she couldn't afford to think about it! She was lucky she had the presence of mind to retreat with her dignity intact.

"Maybe tomorrow night?" Parker called.

That was exactly what she needed. A whole day to prepare her nerves for a whole evening with him. "Sounds good," she called. "Tomorrow."

She ended up going to a movie and driving through a take-out place. She sat nibbling a couple of card-board-tasting tacos in the well-lit parking lot of the fast-food chain.

Whatever Flo had fixed would have been much better, she thought, tossing what was left of the second taco into the sack beside her on the pickup seat.

She stared vacantly at the busy street in front of her. What was she going to do? Everything she did backfired.

She'd lectured him about paying attention to his friends and suddenly, he was paying way too much attention. In his attentive state, nothing much got past him.

She'd suggested he get contacts and a new hairstyle and now, instead of just making her heart beat fast, he also made her knees shake and breathing impossible. She was in a constant state of wishing he would kiss her again.

She'd helped him buy clothes that hugged his body as if they were made specifically to show her how well he'd fine-tuned it. Now she couldn't look at him without wishing he would press her against it. Fat lot of chance she had to kill her feelings for him at this rate.

Like a total idiot, she'd moved into his house with him, insuring that she'd have to see him every day instead of once every few weeks when he thought to show up. Dumb. And dumber to stay.

In two weeks, she'd furnished the major rooms—the living room, dining room, one of the study/den-type rooms and two of the seven bedrooms. She was done with those except for the last few accessories, and she'd wanted to take Parker shopping with her for those. He could afford some really good pieces of art. Since the kinds of things she had in mind would be investments as well as accents, she'd wanted his input. He should choose things he really liked.

After the drapes were delivered and hung tomorrow, he'd be almost ready for the party he was hosting.

The big family room downstairs was the only room left that had to be prepared for that. It was huge, had a bar at one end and room for a couple of pool tables as well as three or four seating areas. Parker had indicated that he hoped to entertain the majority of his classmates there. The wall of walk-out glass doors would also give access to the large expanse of deck and patio outside. She'd have to get outdoor furnishings, too. She could leave when all that area was in shape, too.

She knew exactly what she wanted. With a little hustle, she could find it all fairly quickly. In a couple of days, she could declare his house finished. It shouldn't be hard to convince him he didn't need to furnish bedrooms no one would see. Then she could move out.

To where? That stopped her cold. She hadn't looked at houses yet. She'd planned to do that while she worked on his house. She'd been caught up and hadn't even thought of it.

And if she found a house tomorrow, it usually took a minimum of thirty days to go through the whole procedure and close. Especially since she'd have to find a new banker.

Yeah, Rob had told her dating him wouldn't affect their business relationship. But she'd seen the way he looked at her when she told him last night she wasn't planning on seeing him again. Rob wouldn't deny her future loans, but asking for them would just be too awkward. Awkward and uncomfortable.

But she *hated* the awkwardness of change, too. She absolutely hated the idea of reestablishing herself with a new loan officer. Convincing the first one—Rob—that a lone woman was capable of remodeling houses for a profit had been a big enough trick.

Way to go, Cindy! You could give lessons in how to do a favor for a friend and ruin your life.

She mentally made a list: Things To Do To Get My Life Back On Track. Tomorrow she'd call Monique and look in earnest for a house to be her next project. By evening, she *would* have something in the works. With the extra money she was making from Parker, maybe she'd be able to hurry things through the way her last buyers had.

Maybe in two weeks—time enough to do the family room, even if she had to special order things—she'd be out of Parker's house. In the meantime—well, except for the 'fancy' dinner tomorrow night, which she'd already agreed to—she'd keep her distance.

But darn it! Why should Mallory have Parker?

Cindy inadvertently mashed the paper cup in her hand, spewing crushed ice all over her. With a grimace, she climbed out of her truck and brushed ice off her and out of the pickup. After using a napkin to dry off the seat, she carried her trash to the receptacle on the other side of the parking lot. Feeling calmer—the ice shower had cooled her down, the mindless activity had soothed her a bit—she climbed back in. But she still didn't go anywhere.

Why *should* Mallory have Parker? She didn't even know she was in the race. She'd had a lot of years to want him, but she hadn't. She didn't know he wanted her. What made her sister more worthy of Parker Chaney than *she* was?

Gnawing on her lip, she rested her chin on the forearms she draped over the top of the steering wheel. She'd spent the years since high school avoiding anything unfamiliar while waiting for Parker to discover that he, too, was head over heels in love with her. Maybe, instead of giving up automatically as she had the moment Parker had told her he wanted Mallory, she should fight for her dreams.

In a few months, Mallory would be here and all Cindy's chances would be gone. There would never be a better time. All her life, she'd gone to unbelievable extremes to avoid making a fool of herself. What if humiliation was all she achieved?

She closed her eyes and remembered the way his kisses had felt. With no effort at all, she could feel again the lightness and joy in her soul when he'd danced her around the sidewalk.

Pride. Small price when she had everything— Parker—to gain.

But pride wasn't what had held her back this long, she finally admitted. Even now when she was trying to be brutally honest, she shied away from the question battering her.

What if she found out Parker could *never* love her?

That's what had kept her waiting, silently, patiently, all this time. She wasn't sure she could take the pain. But that was no longer the question. Now it had become, could she take the pain of never knowing?

Maybe it was time—once and for all—to find out.

CHAPTER NINE

CINDY was lost in a mental fog of planning her attack as she pulled around the curve in Parker's driveway. The sound of her name wafted in her open window as she headed her little pickup down the hill toward the carport that sheltered the staff entrance to his house.

Cindy stepped on the brake lightly, looked around, then decided her imagination was working overtime.

"Cindy," someone hollered again as she was ready to press her foot on the gas pedal again. Cindy checked the rearview mirror as a familiar image ran toward her.

Objects Are Closer Than They Appear the wording on the mirror mocked Cindy. *This* object was supposed to be a thousand miles away but it only took one glimpse to know she wasn't hallucinating.

Cindy jammed the brakes and was out, sprinting toward Mallory before the truck quit rocking from the sudden stop.

"What are you doing here?" she asked as they enfolded each other in a warm hug.

"Which reason do you want?" Mallory asked. "You've sounded strange the last few times we've talked. I've been a little homesick—Lord knows what for," she added with a light laugh. "I thought it was time," she finished. "Take your pick."

Over Mallory's shoulder, Parker stood watching them from beneath the chandelier-type porch fixture.

There was a luxury-size rental car sitting in the circular driveway. As Cindy started herding Mallory toward the front porch, an idiotic refrain from *Through The Looking Glass* played in her head. *I'm late. I'm late. For a very important date.* With a sinking feeling that didn't stop until it got to her toes, Cindy realized she was too late. She'd waited too long. With Mallory here, her chances were gone.

"She got here a few minutes ago," Parker explained as Cindy accompanied him to retrieve Mallory's suitcases from the car. "We hadn't made it into the house yet when we saw you pulling in."

"I wanted to come weeks ago," Mallory said a few minutes later as Parker escorted them down the two steps from the oversize foyer into the sunken living room. "She talked me out of it." She shot Cindy a teasing, reproachful look. "I was afraid you'd talk me out of it again if I warned you."

"Since when could I talk you out of anything," Cindy pointed out dryly. "I was in the process of selling my house and moving. I didn't even know where *I* was going to be. Inviting company seemed like really bad timing."

"Oh, I'm company now." Mallory's attractive pout changed to a bright smile before Cindy could respond. "I should have known you'd end up here with PC. He's been coming to our rescue—our very own hero—since we were kids."

He smiled but looked skeptical of her description of him. Cindy felt an inexplicable pride that he wasn't as easily taken in as he used to be.

"Thanks for inviting me to stay," Mallory continued, gazing around. "It isn't like you don't have room for both of us." She turned back to Cindy.

"You told me he'd bought a house. You didn't tell me he'd set himself up in a friggin' mansion." She cleaned up her hip California vocabulary for the benefit of Parker's Midwest living room.

Meticulous in his own choice of words, Parker viewed people who used shock language as too lazy to find the appropriate words to express themselves. Mallory had delighted in riling him frequently during their growing-up years. Her failure to try it now proved she'd either grown up or that she wanted to impress him, Cindy decided.

"I told you the house was huge." Despite the strong bond of affection linking her to both of them, Cindy fought the urge to go pack her bags and run in the other direction.

"You didn't mention that Parker had changed so much, either."

Mallory wanted to impress him, Cindy decided as her sister flounced over to stand in front of him. Rearranging the short strand of hair falling over his forehead, she tilted her head. "Do you know you turned into quite a hunk?" she asked, contradicting her we'll-talk-about-him-as-if-he-isn't-here tone of a moment ago. She pressed a carefully manicured finger on his arm and smiled up at him.

"So I've heard." Instead of looking pleased as Cindy expected, he carefully sidestepped Mallory. "Can I get you both something to drink?" He moved to a bar separating this part of the room from the kitchen and dining area.

Mallory followed him and settled on one of the bar stools. Propping her elbow on the marble counter, she ordered white wine. "Poor PC wasn't quite sure what to do with me, showing up on his doorstep like that."

He poured a glass of wine and lifted it in Cindy's direction before handing it over to Mallory. His expression seemed to mock her earlier assertion that he was almost perfect. Obviously Mallory didn't agree. "What can I get you, Cindy?"

She waved a hand to decline anything, then changed her mind. "Iced tea would be good."

Mallory rolled her eyes and sent Parker an amused smile at her sister's lack of sophistication. It faded on her lips when he poured a second glass from the pitcher Flo kept filled and in the refrigerator beneath the bar. "You going to join us, Cindy?" His intimate smile took her by surprise. "Or maybe you want me to deliver this on a silver platter?"

"Would you?" Cindy asked sweetly, but she wandered over toward them, feeling less like a fifth wheel than she had a few moments before.

"All this luxury's gone to her head," Mallory joked with Parker. "It certainly would mine." She frowned. "Where's your staff? You do have a staff, don't you?"

He laughed as Cindy took one of the comfortable upholstered bar stools she'd bought only a week ago. "I guess you could call it that. Flo's working for me."

"Flo? Our old Flo? From the neighborhood?"

Parker stunned Cindy again by settling in the seat beside her instead of opting for the stool she'd left vacant between her and Mallory. He nodded at Mallory's question.

"Oh? Where is she?" Mallory hinted at rising.

"She's gone to bed, I imagine. She made it clear from the start that she didn't intend to work past nine," he added, with a chuckle.

"That's all? Just Flo?"

"She's all I need. When Cindy moved in, I thought it might be too much additional work for Flo." He winked at Cindy and laid an arm over the back of her chair. The intimate way he said "moved in" made Mallory's carefully shaped eyebrows almost compress above her nose. "But Cindy won't even share the meals Flo prepares for me. She insists on being independent."

"I'm an employee," Cindy protested, partly for Mallory, and partly for his benefit. Cindy had been wary of getting too comfortable with the living arrangements. She'd struggled to keep it a matter of borrowing a section of his house while she was homeless and working on his. She'd worked hard at keeping her role that of "favored" employee.

At the end of the day when Parker came home and found her, she'd update him on her progress, plans and the discoveries she'd made. Then, despite Flo's initial attempts to get her to join Parker for dinner, she'd hurry to her own rooms. "I'm *part* of the staff, not a guest here," she reiterated for him.

He held her gaze, both of his brows raised. "I'll keep that in mind when I hire temporary 'staff' for the reunion thing. I kinda thought we were friends," he added softly before he went on to explain their plans to Mallory.

"Jeez, PC, our class sure blew it when we cast our Most Likely To Succeed votes, didn't we?"

"I guess it depends on what you consider success," he said smoothly, gesturing with one hand, brushing against Cindy's shoulder. "Who *did* earn that honor in the yearbook?"

The way he asked, Cindy knew he already had the

answer but was enjoying playing the game. She wasn't surprised when Mallory said Bill Baxter's name. It was entertaining to watch as they launched into a discussion of others in their high school class. Cindy only half listened as she marveled at Parker, exhibiting up close and personal, the polished master-of-all-he-surveyed qualities she'd seen in his TV interviews or when she'd visited his offices.

Mallory still couldn't decide what to think. She wavered between flirting with the man she'd pretty much ignored as a boy and trying to treat him as if she was his benevolent big sister. It would have been amusing if it wasn't so irritating.

When Cindy couldn't watch any longer, she poked at the ice cubes in her glass and tuned them out. Maybe too much. Her eyes met Parker's when he finally grasped her arm, tightening his grip as he said her name and she realized he must be saying it for the umpteenth time.

"You in there, kid?" He waved a hand in front of her face.

"Kid." That's what he'd called her while he'd been tagging along with her and her dad, before he'd elevated her to "friend" about the time she passed puberty. "What?" she snapped.

"You haven't given up daydreaming, I see," Mallory said blandly.

"I asked where we're going to put Mallory? You know, better than I, what room might be ready for guests."

Kid. Now back to favored employee.

"I'm really impressed with what I've seen so far, Cindy. You're doing a nice job furnishing this house," Mallory said.

Some need to torture herself made Cindy ask. "You wouldn't change anything?"

Mallory wrinkled her nose. "Well. Not much. You're going to let me help, aren't you?"

You can do it, Cindy wanted to say. Instead she shrugged. "I suppose that's up to PC."

He eased from his chair beside her.

"You're going to give me the royal tour?" Mallory asked, rising, too.

"Not me." He held up his hands. "I have to get to bed. Meetings in Chicago tomorrow," he explained to Cindy, "I'd meant to tell you tonight before you went out. Didn't get much chance."

Why? Why are you telling me at all? What in the heck was he doing?

"Which room did you want me to put her luggage in?" He subtly asked Cindy for an answer to his original question.

"First room on the right at the top of the stairs— if that's okay with you," she added. "It's ready. Flo even put some towels in that bathroom when I was showing her some of the accessories I'd bought the other day."

"You aren't going to show me the house then?" Mallory asked.

"Cindy can show you around whenever she wants. You two stay up. Catch up. Do whatever you do. The house is yours," he added directly to Cindy again, as if he was trying to convey some particular meaning. "It's nice to have you here, Mallory." Parker suppressed a yawn. "You're welcome to stay with Cindy as long as you want."

"Thanks," Mallory told him, batting her eyes.

"I'm glad to have…I'm glad we both have such a wonderful refuge," she amended to include Cindy.

Parker blinked twice. Cindy could almost see him repressing some smart remark fermenting in that quick mind. She didn't know whether to be disappointed or relieved when he didn't say whatever it was. "You'll excuse me for tonight?" He nodded to each of them, then headed for his suite of rooms.

"When will you be back from Chicago?" Mallory called.

"As soon as my meeting is over tomorrow," he commented without slowing or turning around. He did stop when he got to the short hall that would lead him to his rooms. "We're still on for dinner tomorrow night?" There was no doubt who he directed the invitation to.

Cindy gaped at him without speaking, then nodded.

"Good night." He saluted both of them.

"Geminy Christmas, Cindy," Mallory said as soon as he'd turned the corner past the massive fireplace. "Why didn't you tell me about him? I take it he has a company plane since he didn't say any specific time for his return flight. Must be nice. Have you flown anywhere in it? Can you believe this house?"

The rapid-fire questions came too fast to answer until she posed the one Cindy didn't want to answer. "What's going on with the two of you?" Mallory asked with a frown.

Cindy managed to avoid the question and get Mallory settled in her room. Forestalling the promised house tour until tomorrow, she sidestepped Mallory's protests that it was still early, West Coast time. Cindy indicated the clock on the small antique shelf she'd chosen for the room. Flo had enthusiastically stocked the shelves with books. "The rest of us are on Midwest time," she said bluntly. "Read a book."

Then she went to find the answer to the question herself. Hesitating at the door to the sitting room of the master suite, she let herself in and closed it carefully behind her. She didn't give herself time to think about what she was doing as she approached the bedroom door and thumped it determinedly.

She heard a bump and a curse and a second later, Parker opened the door. Squinting and obviously more than half asleep, he rubbed at one eye, squeezed the other shut and reached around the corner to flip the light switch in the sitting room. "What?"

Cindy immediately realized her mistake. In a million years, it wouldn't have occurred to her that he would open the door in his underwear. But then she'd never roused him from his bed.

He stood there boldly while she intently stared past him—at his bed. Averting her eyes landed her attention on his very symmetrical, sensuous belly button and she forced herself to concentrate on the doorjamb and why she'd come.

"*What* is going on with you?" She discovered the perfect place to stare was directly into his sleepy eyes.

"Whaddaya mean?" He roughly wiped one hand over his face as if he was trying to wash the drowsiness away. The action displayed his muscular chest to terrific advantage and she had trouble keeping her focus on his eyes.

"What kind of game are you playing with me now, Parker Chaney?"

He closed one eye again, squinting the other

against the light. "I have to be out of here at five in the morning. Do we have to do this tonight?"

"Yes."

He looked resigned. "Maybe it would help if you explained what you're talking about."

"Do you intend to use me to make Mal jealous?" she demanded.

"What?" He yawned, stretching lazily, flexing muscles she didn't know he had, flattening his belly where the swath of soft hair turned into a thin line and meandered slowly toward...

Good grief. What was she doing looking there?

Forcing her gaze back to his face, she realized he was alert and a whole lot more awake now...and greatly amused. He reached past her, grabbing a wool throw from the back of the rocking chair in his sitting room and wrapped it around his waist, tying it in a clumsy loose knot at his side. "That better?" he asked.

"A little. Can't you afford a robe?" she asked irritably.

"I live in a ten thousand square foot house, mostly by myself," he added with a grimace. "Why do I need a robe? Who's going to see me?" He grinned. "Except you, of course, when you decide to come to my bedroom in the middle of the night." He angled his head. "Now what was it you wanted to talk about?"

What was she doing here? Finding answers, she reminded herself and determined she was not going to be distracted or waylaid from that goal. "Is your plan to use me to make Mallory jealous?" she asked again.

"I don't have a plan," he denied. "I didn't know

your sister was coming here tonight. Did you?'' He didn't wait for a response. ''How could I make a 'plan' involving her?''

''But you do intend to marry—''

''I've been trying to tell you for weeks—'' he shook his head in exasperation ''—that is off. What is that Bible verse? 'When I became a man, I put away childish things'?'' He propped himself against the doorjamb with his bare forearm. ''*That* plan was some childish fantasy I hadn't thought about in years. I dug it out again when I got the fifteenth reunion invitation and remembered my plan to be married by now. Maybe because I haven't had time to think about marriage since then, I dusted off some youthful desire and thought I could polish it up and pretend it was new. I thought *you* could polish me up to fit some idealistic image from way back when. That's all it was. An image. It was based on nothing but I hadn't replaced it with anything else so.... The current plan—if you want to call it that—is to sit back and see what happens.''

''Then you've changed your mind? You don't want to get married?''

Placing a finger beneath her chin, Parker lowered his voice and lifted her face. ''I didn't say that, now did I?''

He studied her then let the back of his finger follow the line of her jaw. Slowly, back and forth. She wanted to curl into his hand, into him.

''After reevaluating my status and goals,'' he continued, ''I've resolved to be more prudent in my approach to the marriage thing.''

He was sending pleasant sensations to various points of her body with his light touch. He traced the line of her neck, paying special attention to her collarbone. She wanted to laugh. How could he stand there in his underwear with some colorful Indian print wrapped around him, spouting what sounded like business philosophy in a discussion about marriage?

"Don't you think it's wise to use a little common sense and caution instead of approaching marriage using a seventeen year old's outdated game plan?"

Common sense? How could she think about common sense? All she wanted to do was step between his widely planted bare feet, press into the warmth of his chest, close her heavy eyelids and raise her head. She wanted to see what would happen.

Maybe whatever happened would answer Mallory's question; what was going on between them?

She managed to do the opposite of what she wanted to and stepped back, away from his touch. She had to be able to think. "I..." She shook her head to clear it and tried to remember his question. He didn't think it was wise to use an outdated game plan. "Surely there's something to be said about youthful idealism. It got you where you are now."

He crossed his arms over his sculpted chest. "But fortunately, I'm not the same as I was then. My motives have changed, for one thing."

"Your motives?"

"Yeah. My motives then had more to do with proving something—to myself and everyone else. Now I've proven myself to my satisfaction and what everyone else thinks doesn't matter. It's a nice feeling. Now it's just a challenge to make computers easier to use, make people's lives better, help them work more efficiently. And keep my employees employed."

"And make money?" she asked.

"That's a by-product." He curled the corner of his mouth. "A nice one, I'll admit. But it's important that whoever I marry—if I get married—thinks it's a by-product, too. A little extra bonus besides having me." He looked downright cocky as he seemed to wait to see if that had sunk in. "With certain people, that would cause me qualms from time to time. Surely I don't need the additional speculation about whether the woman I marry loves me or some polished image of me. What's she going to think when she finds out the truth. You can't live with someone day after day without finding out some truths, do you think?"

What truths? He was looking at her with a little too much speculation. "Then you should marry someone who's always cared about you, even before your success." Argh! Why'd she say that?

His smile spread slowly. She looked down at the hands she'd twisted together. "Mallory's known you before and after," she rushed to distract him from whatever he might be thinking. "Maybe that's why the old plan's a good one."

"That wasn't your initial reaction when I told it to you."

What had she said? She searched her mind. All she could remember was the desperate, desolate pain, feeling like her world had come to an end.

She shrugged. "You're allowed mistakes in judgment. Why shouldn't I have the same right?"

"Those kind of mistakes can mess up your life. The key to not letting them is how quickly you correct them," he philosophized, but the words held an edge.

She couldn't think of anything to answer. After a moment of feeling like she was under some kind of powerful microscope, she said, "Thanks for asking Mallory to stay. She's sort of my guest, she could have stayed with me, in my little set of rooms."

"You only have one bed," he commented as if the thought was unimaginable.

"It wouldn't be the first time Mallory and I have shared," Cindy said. "We're sisters. I guarantee it wouldn't have hurt either of us."

"Too bad you already furnished some of the bedrooms," he lowered his voice seductively. "One of you could have shared with me." The teasing note in his voice didn't match the look in his eyes. The longing there slammed her back to the night a couple of weeks ago. He'd said he wanted her. She didn't need his kisses to make her mouth water. She didn't need to feel him pressed against her for the heat to rise in the pit of her stomach and spread languidly through her body. Memory did it all. She forced herself to focus on the first part of what he'd said.

"I've decided not to furnish any more of the bedrooms. You'll be glad to know I'm going house hunting tomorrow. With a little luck, I should be outta here in a couple of weeks, a month at the latest."

He straightened. "You're going to leave with my house half-finished?"

"Of course not. But I'll be finished with everything but a few of the bed—"

"You think I offered what I'm paying you so you could only do the job halfway?"

His reaction so startled her she let her jaw fall open. "You want me to do all the bedrooms? Everything?"

"Everything."

"Won't that be a waste of money and time? You may decide you want to have kids right away. Mal—

your wife," she amended when he opened his mouth to correct her, "will want to redo them. You'll want a nursery—"

"Maybe you should let me decide when and if I want to have kids," he stopped her.

"Maybe you should include your wife in that kind of decision," she said defiantly.

"Gotta have one before I can include her in any decisions," he said. "Hey." He snapped his fingers. "Maybe you should take that on. Maybe you'd carry out your part of the bargain that way. I'd get my house done and a wife. What a bonus."

She wanted to slap him. Some time in this conversation, he'd stepped closer and the heat from his bare chest pressed against her, driving all the air from her lungs. Oh criminy, he did know too much. "I don't think that's funny."

"It's logical. Don't you think? You fit all the requirements we've talked about." His rational tone cut. "You knew me before my transformation. You liked me when I was broke, haven't tried to take advantage since I've made money. You liked me when I was a high-school disaster as much as you do now that I'm a world-class success."

"I liked you better," she snipped.

That seemed to leave him speechless. A hint of anger glinted in his eyes.

"You weren't cruel then," she added in a murmur.

"How is asking you to marry me being cruel?" His bewilderment seemed genuine.

"Oh, is that what that was." She made a face at him. "That proposal was as real as all the attention you were showing me tonight. Right? None of it was for Mallory's benefit?"

"I'd say it's the other way around. Mallory showing up was beneficial."

Cindy scowled up at him.

"For once, to be polite to your sister, you had to stick around for more than a fifteen-minute daily progress report."

"Oh." Her mind was blank.

"What's happened to us, Cindy?" The arms he'd kept folded tightly across his chest for most of their conversation wrapped around her and alarm bells went off in her head. "Things have changed between us, but—"

"Nothing's changed for me." She flattened her hands against his chest as he drew her closer and pushed herself away. "Save your Casanova act for Mallory."

He let her go as if she'd punched him in the gut.

"I'm tired of being practiced on and she doesn't know you well enough to know it's all an act," she added for good measure. "Even if she did, playing let's pretend is one of her favorite things."

A muscle in the side of Parker's face jutted like a granite boulder.

"The two of you will get—"

The gleam in his blue eyes dulled as he quietly shut the bedroom door in her face.

"—along just fine."

CHAPTER TEN

WHAT had she done?

Cindy stumbled across his sitting room to the circular stairway that led down to his exercise room and the basement beyond. What had she done?

She'd never seen a look quite so pained in Parker's eyes. Even when his mother had died. But he'd known that was coming. It had been a long illness and almost a release when he knew she was no longer suffering.

By the time she reached her little apartment at the other end of the house, she no longer suspected, she *knew* she was a fool. Parker was right. Lots had changed between them. Lots that she'd prayed and waited and wished for. He'd offered to marry her. And she'd thrown it back in his face.

"Offered. That's the problem," she muttered as she stalked around her small sitting room, flopping down on the couch then getting up again. *Logically! He'd offered logically.*

But what other way was he going to offer, Cindy wondered.

He could *ask* her. With love instead of logic. Oh, no, he hadn't mentioned *that* word.

She'd resented him wanting to change for Mallory. Why should she expect him to change for her? Then he wouldn't be Parker, would he? something inside her defended him. The Parker she loved.

It had only been a few short hours since she'd sat

at the taco place and resolved to win his love. What had happened?

Mallory had shown up! Cindy answered her own question and knew the fragment of the envy she carried with her when Mallory was around was still firmly embedded in her mind.

Poor Mallory. She'd had her own crosses to bear. She'd always been a little jealous of Cindy's close relationship with their father. Since their parents had died, she'd never stopped searching for a new and more devoted one to take his place.

As sure as Parker could fill the role for a while, he wouldn't be as attentive as Mallory needed over the long haul. She'd be doing both Parker and Mallory a favor—and it would serve Parker right—if she stomped back up to his room and took him up on his offer.

But she couldn't fulfill Parker's needs. Could she?

She'd seriously stunted her growth for so long, could she grow and become the kind of wife a man like Parker Chaney needed?

With the pain in her heart so sharp, she didn't even try to lie down and sleep. At three in the morning, her head came up with a plan and her heart reluctantly agreed it had no choice but to go along.

If she could pull *this* off, she'd know she could be the wife Parker deserved and needed.

She was waiting in the foyer when Parker emerged from his rooms at a quarter to five in the morning. He stutter-stepped the moment he saw her, then straightened his shoulders and came toward her.

"I didn't expect you to be up at this hour of the morning." His voice was carefully flat. His eyes toured her body and obviously noted that she wasn't wearing work garb—she'd put on the little black dress and heels—but he didn't comment.

"I...I hoped you'd let me hitch a ride with you to Chicago."

His eyebrows raised as he gave voice to the wariness clouding his eyes. "If you want to talk about las—"

"There's a huge furniture distributor I've been hearing about in Chicago." She motioned toward the living room. "I've bought several of their things but the selection is kind of limited locally. I thought if I could see everything..." His reserved stare was making it difficult to think. "I might be able to...to...get everything I needed for the family room downstairs in one place. If I just went there," she added and knew she was losing her nerve.

Obviously still perplexed by the request, he warned, "I won't be there all that long."

"I know exactly what I want." She forced herself to hold her gaze steady. "It won't take me long to find out if it's available."

He gestured with his hand. "Whatever." He was the one who looked away, glancing down at his watch. She saw dark circles beneath his eyes with his head lowered and knowing they matched hers eased her mind a little.

"I arranged for the limo to pick me...us up. Ted should be here in about five minutes." PC, Inc.'s driver always picked him up when he had to go to the airport. She suspected he was telling her now to have something to say.

"Lemme get my things." She dashed for the winding stairs. She didn't have much time to do what she needed but knowing the house well helped. Though he wasn't exactly ecstatic at the thought of her going, she didn't think he'd leave without her.

When she returned, she was panting and wishing she'd stopped to take off the heels and carry them instead of wearing them. She was glad she didn't when she saw Mallory standing beside him. How could she look beautiful, straight out of bed, this early in the morning?

Mallory's elegant dressing robe she'd left open to the waist. It swept the floor as she moved. One tiny pearlized button was fastened there. The matching gown beneath it wasn't transparent but it wasn't exactly modest, either. And the coffee and cream color made her dark hair gleam like satin against it.

Parker looked a little more at ease. They both looked up as Cindy approached them.

"What are you doing up so early?" Cindy asked.

"I was having trouble sleeping." Mallory grimaced. "It's not much past my normal bedtime at home."

Cindy could see Parker automatically do the Pacific Time calculations. "What time do you get up in the morning then," he asked.

"Around noon," Mallory said. "Nothing important happens before then, anyway." She looked Cindy up and down. "You look great, sis. Is that the dress I told you to buy for Rob?" Somehow, the words sounded derogatory though Cindy couldn't say why. Mallory didn't wait for an answer. "When did you decide to go to Chicago with PC?"

"Last night after I went to bed." She could feel Parker's gaze on her. "I'm sorry. I know it's your first day here but you're going to be around for a while. Right? I didn't know when I'd get another chance. I left you a note.''

"Hey. Why don't I go, too? We'll have a wonderful time picking out furniture together." She draped an arm through Parker's. "PC can help us when he's finished with whatever he has to do. Wouldn't that be fun? We could—"

"Sorry, Mal. We don't have time," he interrupted. Parker took the bag from Cindy and lightly clasped her arm with the other hand. "Ted's already waiting outside," he said to Cindy.

"It's your own plane." Mallory imitated a pout. "Can't you go whenever you want?"

"I have meetings. I don't intend to be late." He tugged Cindy toward the door. "We'll probably be back by the time you're up for the day anyway," he added over his shoulder. But he didn't look back and he looked amused.

Not letting go of her arm, he lifted Cindy's duffel bag to indicate she should open the front door. He smiled down at her. "We aren't going to be there that long you know," he warned again, hefting her bag.

Ted came around to open the limo door. "Long enough, I hope," she muttered as she got in.

"Long enough," he repeated.

For no reason whatsoever, she found the tingling sensation his fingers left behind when he released her arm encouraging.

The corporate jet's furnishings were about half as pretentious as she'd imagined and about twice as private. Up front, a wall separated them from the cockpit. Parker had introduced her to the pilot and his one-man crew when they'd come on board and then closed the door between them.

There were three seating groups in the midsize main cabin: one with a table; one with a desk and workspace; and one with conversational-type seating with a curved couch-type thing in the corner with two easy chairs across from it. Parker indicated she should take one of those seats.

Another wall toward the back blocked off a bedroom. Parker hadn't shown her that, just told her. As she'd fastened her seat belt, he brought her a large cup of coffee from the small galley huddled to one side of the cockpit. The pilot had everything ready when they arrived. They were already speeding down the runway.

She heard him settle into the chair at an angle from hers, heard the metallic click of his seat belt. She fiddled with getting the cup into the holder he had shown her, glanced around the comfortable cabin one more time and finally looked at him, blaming the flutter in her stomach on the small jet lifting off the ground.

He was calmly staring at her as if waiting for her attention.

"Why this time?" he asked without preamble. "Why now when you haven't accepted any of my invitations to come with me before?"

"Why this time *without* an invitation, you mean?" Cindy asked lightly.

"Okay. Say it that way if you prefer."

He wasn't going to make this easy. And he certainly planned to force her hand before they'd spent too much of the day. He'd told her his day's agenda on the ride to the small private airport and she'd tentatively slotted the time for her "deed" as on the way home.

What if it didn't go well? Her palms were already sweaty. She'd be stuck and at his mercy in some strange unfamiliar territory for as long as he wanted to torture her.

"I've never needed to buy you furniture before."

His one raised eyebrow told her that didn't wash. He hadn't even waited to look skeptical until she'd finished.

His expression went back to looking grim. "Why is it that you're coming with me to Chicago, Cindy?" he asked again quietly.

"I—"

The crewman's voice rescued her as he said over the speaker that they'd reached cruising altitude and they were free to move around as they wished. "It'll be a little over an hour flight," he added. "Let me know if you need anything."

"I need—" Cindy unfastened her seat belt and glanced around her. "I need my bag. What'd you do with my duffel bag?" She gathered as much courage as she ever would. It was time to get it over with.

Parker was a little slower releasing himself from his seat. "It can't have anything too important in it," he said frowning as he went to a small cabinet by the door and got it out. "It's too—" he shook it before handing it over "—light."

"It's *very* important." She wanted to hug the bag to her. "Now you sit down." She pointed him back to his chair.

"Getting a little bossy, aren't we," he said as she turned her back on him. His voice held the fond amusement she'd grown to expect and anticipate over the years.

She set the bag on the small end table and unzipped

it. Her eyes were so damp with emotion-filled tears she couldn't see what she had inside. But she knew and her mouth went dry.

She'd planned what to say. But she hadn't planned how to say it or what to do. All she knew was worst case: she'd know where she stood and finally be able to deal with it because she'd given it her best shot. Best case: he'd been serious last night and she'd *love* where she stood and have her whole life to learn to deal with him loving her.

She swung back toward him, her hands behind her, gripping the edge of the small table. "Last night, did you..." She took a deep breath. "Do you...were you..."

"Are we going to practice conjugating things?" He rose, stepping toward her as the plane lurched and she fell forward. "Air pocket," he explained, catching her. He braced her against his chest while she stabilized then held her an arm's length away. "You're crying," he exclaimed, letting go of one arm to gently thumb away the moisture under her eye.

"No, I'm not," she protested. "It isn't...I'm not... You can't..."

"If we're going to stand around and do this conjugating thing, I can think of better things to conjugate than infinitives." His head came down, his lips touched hers in a reverent kiss that stopped her heart.

Suddenly she *was* crying—and laughing at the same time. There was nothing logical about it and everything felt like love. She tried to push him away but his arms tightened. "Don't. Don't act like you don't like that. I won't believe it."

"I love it," she protested, too breathless to laugh, too weak to struggle but trying to push him away anyway. "But you have to let me do something. I…you asked why I wanted to come with you. Please, you have to let me do this."

He let her shove him into his seat. The look on his face made it difficult to turn away to retrieve her treasures from the bag. Taking a deep breath, she managed it. "If the shoe fits, will you wear it?" she asked over her shoulder, then turned back around.

His frown was a bemused one.

"Say you will," she prompted, still keeping her hands behind her back.

"If the shoe fits, I'll wear it," he agreed.

She bent to her knees, setting his favorite battered running shoes down on either side of him. He started to pull his foot away when she tried to remove the nice dress shoes he'd put on.

"It's okay, PC," she said affectionately. "I already know you have flat feet."

He relaxed, granting her a magnificent smile when she looked at him. "Isn't it cheating—" he bent and placed a quick peck on her mouth "—to borrow shoes you know are going to fit and then ask if I'll wear them?"

"I've been playing fair way too long," she mumbled, moving the dress shoes out of her way. "You should have seen me sprinting through the basement and sneaking into your room to get them this morning while you were waiting in the foyer. Put your foot in here," she ordered, holding up the flap of the first shoe. "I was terrified you'd thrown them away," she added between clenched teeth as she struggled to push the first one on.

"It's a good thing you didn't decide to become a shoe salesman." He stood, pushing his foot the rest of the way in and pulling her up and into his arms at the same time. "What's the point?"

He didn't give her a chance to answer as his mouth covered hers. A shared sigh mingled and she savored it as she inhaled it on a deep sigh. She felt too weak to hold her head up when he finally lifted his. She sagged against his chest.

"What's the point?" he asked again, nuzzling tiny kisses along her neck, around her face, on her eyelids. "Of the shoes," he added when she scowled, totally perplexed.

She smiled, still too blissfully happy to want to think. "We have to put the other one on." She didn't make any move in that direction. That would mean she'd have to leave his arms. "If it fits, I can declare you Prince Charming. After that list," she added, "I wanted to show you you've always been Prince Charming to me."

"Always?" A bit of skepticism filtered into his tone.

"As long as I can remember," she said. "A whole lot longer than was sane." She sobered, drawing a little away until he drew her back.

"Why didn't you bring me to my senses?"

"I tried from time to time," she whispered. "Remember when I asked you to teach me to kiss?"

"When you were fourteen?"

She nodded. "You wouldn't even kiss me once."

He laughed. "I was terrified," he admitted. "You were very, very well...formed at the time. Do you also remember when you'd come hang out with me, a lot of times I never moved from whatever chair I was in the entire time you were there."

She frowned.

"I thought...I knew," he amended, "that it would be very easy to take advantage of you and your hero-worship thing. And very difficult *not* to. Believe me, I spent a lot of very uncomfortable hours trying hard—I've never been very good at it but that's a pun in case you don't know—not to be turned on by you."

"You were crazy in love with Mallory back then."

"I thought I was," he admitted. "I'm beginning to wonder if I was fooling myself all along."

"What do you mean?" She traced his scrunched eyebrow, smoothing the scowl out.

"She never affected me like you did. Never!"

"Even now?"

He laughed. "If I'd had any doubts before last night, they would have been wiped out the minute she presented herself on my doorstep. I opened the door and looked at her and saw a plastic doll who could be put under a glass dome and set on a shelf. I couldn't even imagine wanting to get her out and play with her."

"Is that another pun?"

He kissed her silly. Just when she was ready to suggest they check out the bedroom in the back, the pilot's voice warned them they'd be landing in five minutes and encouraged them to take their seats and put on their seat belts if they didn't have them on already.

"Damn!" Parker said, putting her reluctantly away.

She straightened her clothes. "Can we both fit in your chair?"

"I have a feeling if we both fit in my chair, my

crew will get a very interesting surprise when they come through that door in about ten minutes.''

Cindy sighed and reluctantly sat down. Parker put on his other shoe, propping it on her leg to prove it fit.

"I declare you Prince Charming," she said just as she'd practiced in her room last night. Then she remembered where their conversation had left off. "How *did* Mallory affect you?" she asked.

"Mallory was like some prize," he said after a thoughtful moment. "Getting her attention became a challenge like…like…getting my computer to do something I'd been struggling to get it to do. It was a euphoric feeling anytime she treated me like something other than the furniture." He grimaced. "If it's any comfort, I still feel the same way about the computers."

"But now? Still? Why—"

"Habit," he said. "I got the invitation and remembered thinking I'd be married by my fifteenth reunion. Mallory popped into my mind. Habit," he said again. "I got so accustomed to thinking marriage and Mallory in the same sentence that it didn't occur to me to think any differently."

"What changed your mind?" she asked quietly, terrified and excited all at once to hear the answer.

"You pointing out that it would change our relationship," he said. "I haven't been able to think the same way since that day. It scared me to think having Mallory would mean I'd have to give you up. In any way."

Both of them stayed patiently lost in their thoughts until the plane bumped down. It seemed to jolt a question from her. "Do you love me?"

His smile grew so slowly she was afraid she'd die from holding her breath. "Do computers compute? Do birds fly? Do...do..."

"Do fishes swim," she supplied for him and then shook her head with exasperation. "Can't you just say it?"

The look he gave her turned her right back into the same unthinking, inanimate object she'd been a few minutes ago in his arms. "Not from here," he said. "Not from here."

He loosened his seat belt and she realized the plane had stopped. With a rush of withering disappointment, she saw him pace toward the other end of the plane. She'd thought he was coming back to her arms.

He said something to the two men in the cockpit and then went to the desk. They were going to have to get on with their day. She supposed knowing this much might make it possible to get through it. She started to release her seat belt.

"Stay there," Parker ordered quietly and turned to speak into the phone he'd dialed.

The pilot and crewman came through the cabin, smiling from ear to ear, exchanging glances. "Ma'am." The pilot lifted his hat and opened the outside door. "We'll do what we can to get going again soon." They both went outside as Parker hung up the phone.

"Come here," he said, holding out his hands as he came toward her.

She didn't know she could move so quickly. When she was back in his arms, he sighed. "Now, what was the question?" he teased. "Oh, yeah. Do I love you?"

She stared up at him, one hand cupping his beloved

face. When she thought she would die and go to a heaven as blue as his eyes if she had to wait any longer, when she thought she couldn't wait another second to hear the words, he finally said, "I don't know" and pulled her tight into his arms.

She groaned aloud.

"I love you if it means I can't stand the thought of not having you in my house where I can find you every day when I get home. I love you if it means I don't want to put on any kind of reunion party if you aren't there by my side to play hostess. I love you if it means the thought of losing even a teeny, tiny bit of our friendship tears something right out of me. I love you if it means I cringe every time you said that other guy's name."

"Rob?"

He cringed and held her tighter. "I love you if it means when I think of babies, I picture ones who look like you. I love you if it means I want to make love to you from now until the end of time."

"Why did you go weeks at a time without seeing me?" she wondered aloud.

"Do you know how many cold showers I've taken over the years?" he asked, laughing and adding another. "I love you if it means I'll never have to take another cold shower. You'll never know how evil I sometimes felt for thinking some of the thoughts I thought about my best friend." He sobered. "I think part of it had to do with your father."

"What do you mean?" With a flash of understanding, she thought she knew. With his own father long gone, he'd admired Sid Johnson almost as much as Cindy had. For as long as she could remember, Parker had tagged around with them. After her parents had died and Aunt Janette had come to live with her and Mallory, Cindy had wondered for a while if she had totally disappeared. Mallory and Aunt Janette were so alike. The same things were important to them. Cindy had felt so alone—then Parker had taken her under his wing. He confirmed her thoughts with his next words. "He'd been so good to me. I felt so responsible for you. The thoughts I had made me feel so guilty, like I was betraying him."

She pulled his face down to hers. "I love you, Parker Chaney," she whispered.

"Good." He kissed her until her toes curled, then set her away from him.

"Your meeting," she remembered.

"I just authorized one of the VPs who's going to be there to act in my stead," he said. "I'm not going."

"Good," it was her turn to say. "You can stay here with me."

"You're not going to buy furniture," he teased. "What about that distributor?"

"Okay. Rub it in. You knew the minute I showed up this morning I wasn't coming for any reason but to be with you."

He shook his head. "At first I thought you were coming to rub it in that you'd refused to marry me."

"You call that a proposal?" she asked. "What was your second thought?" she asked before he could answer.

"I thought maybe we were finally going to get on the same page in this relationship."

What do you mean? her scowl said. Her fingers were tracing every line of his head, his face, his shoulders. The feeling from the tips of them to the bottom of her soul was very possessive.

"I thought for once, maybe we were both going to admit how we felt about each other."

"You knew I loved you all along?" she asked with a strange mixture of pleasure and disappointment.

"I *thought* you did the first time I kissed you. I knew I loved you that night on the Plaza, but then I wasn't sure about you."

"I worked so hard to keep you from discovering all my secrets."

He laughed. "You could have saved us both a lot of trouble if you'd just told me. I count on you to keep me in touch with reality."

"I count on you to keep my head in the clouds," she said, smiling, kissing him, wanting more and more to adjourn to the bed at the back of the plane. The idea of making love with him was becoming a burning need.

"Good. That's exactly what I plan to do," he said, waving on the crew, who had just returned.

"All set," the pilot told him, grinning from ear to ear as he and the crewman made their way to the cockpit. "We're cleared for takeoff as soon as you're ready."

"If we don't want to be shocked by something we might see, I think we'd better close the door," the other one said loudly, then shut the door between them firmly.

"We're going home?" she asked, suddenly sorry she hadn't even glanced out the window at Chicago.

"Well, not exactly." He grimaced. "I'm doing this all wrong. I was supposed to be asking you to marry me while they refueled and made the arrangements for Las Vegas. So we can get married," he added when she didn't say anything.

She waited until he frowned. "If you think *that* was a proposal, you're going to be waiting a long time for an answer."

"I'd get on my knees but then I'd have to let you go," he said.

She waited again. "I don't want you to let me go, but if you think *that* will pass as an invitation to marry you, you'd better think again." Her voice softened. "I need the words, Parker Chaney. I need to know you aren't taking me for granted because you can't have Mallory...or...or anyone else. I need to know *I'm* the prize, that you're—"

He hushed her with a kiss that could have gone on forever had the pilot not asked them to prepare for takeoff and fasten their seat belts.

"My seat," Parker said. "We'll both fit." He drew her down on his lap, extending the belt until it fastened around both of them. Then he looked into her eyes. "I love you with my heart and soul, Cindy. You're such a part of me, I can't imagine life without you. Will you help me create our very own happily ever after?"

She wasn't sure if her heart was soaring or if the plane was taking off as he finally said, "Will you marry me?" The kiss he punctuated it with was long and slow.

When he raised his head, she was bursting with her yes, but he made her laugh instead by saying, "Will that do?"

She snuggled close to his heart. "That'll do."

"Is that supposed to pass for a yes?" he asked after a moment.

"What do you think, my handsome Prince Charming?"

"It'll do."

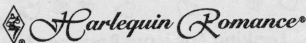

Harlequin Romance®

brings you four very special weddings to remember in our new series:

WHITE WEDDINGS

True love is worth waiting for....

Look out for the following titles by some of your favorite authors:

August 1999—SHOTGUN BRIDEGROOM #3564
Day Leclaire
Everyone is determined to protect Annie's good name and ensure that bad boy Sam's seduction attempts don't end in the bedroom—but begin with a wedding!

September 1999—A WEDDING WORTH WAITING FOR #3569
Jessica Steele
Karrie was smitten by boss Farne Maitland. But she was determined to be a virgin bride. There was only one solution: marry and quickly!

October 1999—MARRYING MR. RIGHT #3573
Carolyn Greene
Greg was wrongly arrested on his wedding night for something he didn't do! Now he's about to reclaim his virgin bride when he discovers Christina's intention to marry someone else....

November 1999—AN INNOCENT BRIDE #3577
Betty Neels
Katrina didn't know it yet but Simon Glenville, the wonderful doctor who'd cared for her sick aunt, was in love with her. When the time was right, he was going to propose....

Available wherever Harlequin books are sold.

HARLEQUIN®
Makes any time special ™

HRWW

Celebrate **15** years with

HARLEQUIN®
Makes any time special ™

In celebration of Harlequin®'s golden anniversary

Enter to win a *dream!* You could win:

- A luxurious trip for two to
  The Renaissance Cottonwoods Resort
  in Scottsdale, Arizona, or

- A bouquet of flowers once a week for a year
  from FTD, or

- A $500 shopping spree, or

- A fabulous bath & body gift basket, including
  K-tel's *Candlelight and Romance* 5-CD set.

Look for **WIN A DREAM** flash on
specially marked Harlequin® titles by
Penny Jordan, Dallas Schulze,
Anne Stuart and Kristine Rolofson
in October 1999*.

FTD

**RENAISSANCE.
COTTONWOODS RESORT**
SCOTTSDALE, ARIZONA

K·TEL

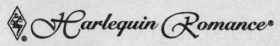

Harlequin Romance®

We're proud to announce the "birth" of a brand-new series full of babies, bachelors and happy-ever-afters: **Daddy Boom.** Meet gorgeous heroes who are about to discover that there's a first time for everything—even fatherhood!

We'll be bringing you one deliciously cute **Daddy Boom** title every other month in 1999. Books in this series are:

February 1999 **BRANNIGAN'S BABY**
Grace Green

April 1999 **DADDY AND DAUGHTERS**
Barbara McMahon

June 1999 **THE DADDY DILEMMA**
Kate Denton

August 1999 **OUTBACK WIFE AND MOTHER**
Barbara Hannay

October 1999 **THE TYCOON'S BABY**
Leigh Michaels

December 1999 **A HUSBAND FOR CHRISTMAS**
Emma Richmond

Who says bachelors and babies don't mix?

Available wherever Harlequin books are sold.

HARLEQUIN®
Makes any time special.™

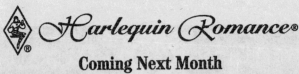

Coming Next Month

#3567 TRIAL ENGAGEMENT Barbara McMahon
It was Mike Black's job to keep Candee safe until she testified in court—
and his idea of protection was hiding out with her at his brother's ranch
and pretending she was his fiancée! Candee was attracted to Mike, but
he knew better than to get involved with her, however hard she was to
resist...

#3568 ONE BRIDE DELIVERED Jeanne Allan
Cheyenne's response to a newspaper advertisement looking for a
mother led her to an orphaned boy and his uncle, Thomas Steele.
Thomas clearly had no place in his life for family or for love. But
Cheyenne knew that if she could draw out the softer side to his nature
he'd make the perfect father—and husband!

Hope Valley Brides: *Four weddings and a family!*

#3569 A WEDDING WORTH WAITING FOR Jessica Steele
Karrie had been the envy of all her colleagues when they found out she
was dating company executive Farne Maitland... But Farne was a man of
the world, while Karrie's upbringing had made her determined to be a
virgin bride. There was only one solution—marry and quickly!

White Weddings: *True love is worth waiting for...*

#3570 AND MOTHER MAKES THREE Liz Fielding
When James Fitzpatrick mistook Bronte for the mother who had
abandoned his little girl, Bronte realized he must have confused her
with her career-minded sister. But James was so handsome, and his
daughter so adorable that Bronte couldn't resist slipping into the role.
What would they do when they discovered that Bronte wasn't quite who
she seemed?